D0680705

I Need Sombody Down For Me 2

Ty Leese Javeh

Ty Leese Javeh

Copyright © 2017 Ty Leese Javeh

All rights reserved.

ISBN: **1545263612**

ISBN-13: **978-1545263617**

DEDICATION

Insert dedication text here. Insert dedication text here. Insert dedication text here. Insert dedication text here. Insert dedication text here. Insert dedication text here. Insert dedication text here. Insert dedication text here. Insert dedication text here. Insert dedication text here.

I Need Somebody Down For Me 2

ACKNOWLEDGMENTS

I give thanks to God for giving me guidance when I needed it the most and for answering my prayers and blessing me with the gift of creativity. But most of all, I thank God for the readers who enjoy my books. I thank Him for my family and friends who always support me and push me to continue to strive for success.

To my publisher, Treasure Malian, thank you for giving me this opportunity. I appreciate you even though there may have been times when you felt as if I didn't. To my sisters—Samantha, Sabrina, Ladonna, and Shanika—I love you guys, and thanks for always being there for me no matter what. To my daughter and granddaughter, Tilysha and Teliyah, it's because of the two of you that I continue to push myself to be better. You are my everything. I love you. To my nieces and nephews—Ricky, Daria, J'Aung, Erin, and Sebyan—Thanks for loving my craziness and for being the best nieces and nephews an aunt can have. To my cousins—Latonya and Andrea—your love, support, and encouragement are greatly appreciated. I love when you inbox me, text me, or call me just to talk about my books; it means a lot to me. To my friends that are more like family—Kesha (Bff), Ashley, Kevin, Sekenah, Tekelia, and Keisha—thank you guys for always encouraging me when I feel frustrated. I love you all. To all my pen sisters, thank you for allowing me to bother you with my doubts and always encouraging and helping me.

My sidekick, T. Nicole: Words can't express the amount of gratitude I have for you. In this short period of time, we went from pen sisters to friends, and now, we are more like sisters. You push me to my limits, and you give me a swift kick in the you-know-what when I need it the most. It's funny how we seem to always be in sync and thinking the same thing. I'm glad to have a beautiful person like you in my corner, cheering me on.

Finally, to the readers, thank you so much for reading my work, following me, and supporting me. I appreciate every one of you. You give me the most encouragement of all. I will continue to strive for success. Words cannot express the feeling of pride I have.

RYDA

Staring into Psycho's eyes, I wasn't looking at the man that I love—the man who took care of me in that hotel room. Yes, he was staring at me with the same look of love as always, but it was something different in his eyes—something more sinister. I looked around at the two dead bodies lying on the floor and the body of the cashier slumped over the counter, trying to figure out what the hell just happened?

"Why you do this to me, Ryda? Don't you know how much I love you?" Psycho questioned in a low voice.

His calm demeanor was scaring the shit out of me. Just moments ago, he burst through the door in a blazing rage. Now, he was totally calm. I was speechless. I slowly turned my head back towards Psycho. His eyes were now narrowed as he glared at me as if he were going to kill me.

"Psycho, we have to go." The desperation in my voice should have snapped him out of what seemed like a trance or something of the sort, but it didn't.

"See what you made me do, Ryda? You let this nigga put his hands all over you. Now, his blood is on yo' hands." He smirked then looked down at the body that was lying at my feet.

I was confused. I had no idea what Psycho was talking about, but I didn't have time to spare having a conversation to try to figure it out. It wasn't even closing time, and anybody could've walked in the store at any given moment.

"Psycho, we can talk about this later, but right now, we have to get the hell out of here," I spoke calmly as I reached for his hand.

"I'm not going nowhere," he replied, snatching his arm away from me.

"Psycho, baby—" I was interrupted by the whimpering sound of the cashier as he fumbled around the counter.   "Fuck!" I shouted, realizing what the cashier had done and knowing that we only had minutes to get the hell out of there.

I snatched the gun out of Psycho's hand and sent two slugs to the cashier's skull, and then, I shot out all the cameras.

I didn't know what the fuck was going on in Psycho's mind, but I needed him to snap out of it quick. With no time to waste, I ran to the back office to retrieve the tape from the security system, thanking God that my former client had ran his mouth about his daily routine, and I knew where the security system was. Hiking up my dress, I used the bottom to turn the knob on the office door.

"Damn it!" I shouted in frustration.

My body started to feel hot as tiny beads of sweat formed on my scalp. I wiped my sweaty palms on my dress.

"Think, Ryda, think," I coached myself as I looked around in a panic.

I noticed the keys dangling from my former client's waist.

"Psycho, grab the keys," I commanded, pointing at the key chain that was hooked onto my former client's belt loop.

Psycho stood frozen with a blank stare on his face. I let out a frustrated sigh as I made a mad dash over to my former client. Careful not to step in the blood that was seeping out of his chest and onto the floor, I used the bottom of my dress to unhook the keys.

"Whatever you're going through, Psycho, snap out of it, now! We have to go!" I snapped. I ran back to the office door, fumbling with the keys as I tried to figure out which one went to the door.

"Shit, shit, shit." None of the keys I'd tried were working.

My heart began racing faster as my adrenaline kicked in; with my heart beating damn near out my chest, fear crept into my body. I tried one last key, and the knob turned. I clasped my hands together in the praying position and thanked God before I rushed into the office, snatched the tape out of the machine, wiped everything down with the bottom of my dress as quickly as possible, and then hauled ass out of the office.

"Come on, Psycho, we got to go, *now!*" I demanded, pulling him by the arm.

"You can't leave me, Ryda. I won't let you," he said in a dead voice, still not budging.

Taking his face in my hands, I looked deeply into his eyes.

"Baby, I'm not going nowhere. I love you." I planted a soft kiss on his lips. "Let's go," I commanded, speaking in a soothing tone.

As if my words breathed life back into Psycho, he snapped out of his trance, grabbed my hand, and rushed out of the door.

"Psycho, give me the keys," I demanded as we made our way to the car.

"I got this," he stated, opening the car door.

"Hurry, Psycho." My heart was pounding as I heard the sirens blaring.

Psycho quickly put the key in the ignition as I put on my seat belt. He started the engine then backed out of the parking space as he turned the steering wheel to the right. I could hear my heart beating loudly over the screeching of tires and the blaring of the sirens.

The police were getting closer; I could see their lights flashing from the parking lot. Psycho whipped the car around so fast that my head almost hit the passenger side window. He put the car into drive and put the pedal to the metal. With the engine roaring like a race car, we sped out of the parking lot.

I don't care if we on the run / Baby, long as I'm next to you / And if loving you is a crime / tell me why do I bring out the best in you/ I hear sirens while we make love.

Beyoncé's voice wailed through the speakers, as the radio was playing "On the Run Part II." I couldn't help but think about how fitting that song was for the moment because I was feeling exactly what Bey was singing. It was as if God were sending me a message. As Jay-Z started rapping his verse, I looked over at Psycho. His eyes were glued to the road with the same emotionless look that he'd had in the store.

"What do you want from me, Ryda?" he asked in a disembodied voice.

I looked at him as if he were a stranger, thinking that the man I loved no longer existed.

"Right now, I just want you to drive this fucking car, and get us home safely." My voice was thick and full of emotions.

Psycho was lost, and I didn't know if I could bring him back to me.

****

We arrived at our apartment, and Psycho seemed to have been in a daze. The awkward silence that we'd ridden home in was deafening. I peeled off my clothes and prepared to shower as I stared, for a second, at the man I loved, wondering what the fuck was going through his head.

I turned on the shower and began washing away my worries. The cool breeze from the bathroom door let me know that Psycho was in the bathroom with me.

Sighing, I spoke. "Baby, what's on your mind, you didn't seem like you were with me tonight," I spoke as I noticed him taking a seat on the toilet, staring at nothing in particular. I quickly washed my body, turned off the water, and then grabbed my towel and wrapped my body as I stepped out to see a withdrawn Psycho.

"Baby, talk to me. What's wrong?" I urged as I caressed the side of his face with my hand.

Looking into my eyes, Psycho's eyes began to well with tears.

"Ryda, I can't lose you. The thought of another man touching what's mine put me in a bad headspace. I can't deal with that shit! You trying to leave me and shit? After everything that we have been through? After me opening up to you? I will fucking kill you, Ryda!"

Psycho pulled out his gun and pressed it against my temple. Thinking this nigga had completely lost his mind, I had to speak fast.

"Baby, what the fuck are you doing? What are you talking about?" I began talking as I noticed the tears leaking from his eyes.

"You were letting him touch you. You was winking and licking your lips and then had the nerve to look at me as if I wasn't shit and went right back to doing that shit in front of me. I told you if you wanted out, you could tell me that shit, but I'm not with that sharing shit. I'll kill you!" he said, and I was lost.

"Baby, I don't know what the fuck you're talking about. None of that shit ever happened. I was casing the place, like we discussed. I was only talking to that man; he never touched me. Baby, look at me! Look! I love you. I would never do anything to disrespect or hurt you. Baby, I'm not sure what's going on with you, but none of that shit happened. It's me; forever your Ryda," I said as I began to get choked up and allow my own tears to fall.

He lowered his gun and pulled me in for an embrace. My heart began to slowly return to its normal pace as I closed my eyes, trying to figure out what the hell was wrong with his ass. This man had a whole damn scene in his head that never happened and tried to kill me over it. If I didn't know he was crazy before, I damn sure knew now.

Psycho looked me in my eyes, apologized, and took me by the hand as he led me to the room. He began to help me lotion my body as he eyed me with love in his eyes. After he'd put his gun away, in its normal spot, I sat up on the bed as he continued to rub my feet.

Wham!

I slapped the shit outta him. "Don't you ever in your fucking life pull a gun out on me again; the next time, you better kill me!" I spat as he looked at me as if he were dazed from the slap I'd just delivered.

After a brief stare down, he apologized again. Then, he began to hug and kiss me until our bodies couldn't take anymore, and we made love until the morning.

Waking up, the bed was empty, and I immediately thought Psycho's crazy ass was up to no damn good, off on some crazy shit. I slipped my feet into my slippers, grabbed my robe, and began to walk around the apartment. Looking out the front window, I noticed that the car was gone and realized that Psycho had left. I began to cook breakfast, as I figured he should be back sooner than later. With bacon, eggs, grits, pancakes, potatoes, and orange juice ready, I heard the front door and peeked around to find a hooded Psycho.

"Baby, where did you go? I didn't hear the car," I stated as I began making his plate and setting things up on the table.

"I left and got rid of the car. I had to walk back. I don't want to take any chances."

"You did what!" I screamed louder than I intended to.

"Calm down. I just don't want to take any chances getting caught with that shit. After thinking about how shit went down last night, I think it's time to do shit differently."

Psycho was talking a good game, but it seemed like he should have waited until we hit a bigger lick before he dumped the car. Now, with no wheels, it was time to devise a plan that would certainly put us in a better place.

"Baby, I know you've been in and out of the streets and have a bit of street smarts, but since we are clearly talking about starting over, things need to change. I've been thinking, and this time, you have no choice but to follow my lead."

Of course, he resisted and didn't like the idea, but at the end of the day, I had his kryptonite, which was my sweet, dripping, always ready honey pot, and with a little convincing, he was ready to listen to our new plan.

PSYCHO

"You think you slick, don't you?" I questioned, slowly stroking Ryda's hair.

She was lying on my chest, recovering from the morning sex we'd just had. She looked up at me with wide eyes, trying to hide the smirk that was threatening to spread across her face.

"What you mean?" she asked innocently, batting her eyes at me, pretending like she didn't know what I was talking about.

I rolled over and mounted my body on top of hers.

"Using yo' bomb ass pussy to try to persuade me. You think that shit work, don't you?" Ryda smiled as she rolled her eyes upwards.

"Let me tell you something; anytime you're offering that shit up, I'ma take it, and as far as yo' plan, the only reason I'm agreeing to it is 'cause I feel like it's something you need to do. However, I have a plan of my own that we must carry out first," I admitted.

"What's your plan?" she asked as I started kissing her neck.

"I'll tell you later. Right now, I wanna try to get some sleep." I gave her a quick kiss then rolled off her.

She returned to her position on my chest, with me stroking her hair, until she drifted off to sleep. A little while later, the sounds of Ryda's light snores let me know that she was deep in her sleep. I chuckled then slowly peeled her off my chest and onto her side of the bed. She squirmed a little, getting comfortable as she snuggled into her pillow. I sat on the side of the bed and ran my hands over my head as I let out a slight sigh. Thoughts of yesterday's events were clouding my mind, making it impossible for me to sleep. I didn't know how in the hell I'd let Cutty get in my head like that. Was I so blinded by my own fucked ass thoughts that I couldn't see through the bullshit?

"Man, Psycho, you must be outta yo' got damn mind," I mumbled to myself as I got up, stretching and scratching my balls.

Sliding my feet into my Nike slides, I adjusted myself in my boxer briefs then headed to the kitchen to grab a beer.

"Fuck outta here, niggas! What the fuck y'all muthafucka's think this is? Joe's Apartment and shit? Y'all better move around before I bomb y'all asses," I said to the roaches that scattered about when I walked into the kitchen.

I walked over to the plates on the table that still held our breakfast on it, picked them up, and then placed them in the sink. I went to the fridge to grab a beer but decided to grab my bottle of 1738 instead. I opened the refrigerator, snatched up my bottle, and then headed back to the bedroom. I picked up my Beats by Dre headphones and my weed box then sat at the foot of the bed and rolled myself a jay as I listened to my old-school playlist. I didn't know what it was about old school music, but it seemed to relax me as well as help me clear my mind. And Lord knew I needed to clear my mind. I had to come up with a plan to get money. After the shit I pulled in the check cashing place, not only did I fuck up that money, but I knew staying in this apartment would definitely make us sitting ducks for the Feds, and I'd rather die than spend my life in a fucking cage.

"Man, fuck that shit, Psycho. You ain't going down like that," I said to myself as I put the blunt in my mouth and lit it up.

After finishing the bottle of 1738 and facing the whole jay, I was fucked up, and I didn't know what the fuck I was doing with the music, but somehow, Gucci Mane and Trey Songz were in my ear talking about *he can lay it down, but I'ma beat it up.* I didn't know if it were the Remy, the weed, or a combination of both, but that song was rockin' like shit at that moment, and it made me want to wake Ryda up so I could slide up in her real quick. I looked over at a sleeping Ryda then smacked her on her ass hard, making her jump up out of her sleep. She looked at me like I was crazy. I flashed her a smile as I rapped along to the lyrics.

Smack it like I'm mad at that / sweaty sex, so passionate / oral sex, she mastered that / pornographic poses like she posin' for the internet.

Ryda was shaking her head and laughing, as I was pointing and moving to the lyrics like I was Gucci Mane himself. Ryda snatched my headphones off.

"Are you seriously into that song like that?" she questioned, shaking her head.

"Hell yeah, Gucci Mane speaks facts; that's me and you, all day. I be doggin' it, straight poundin' it, you know? You throw that ass back; I smack it like I'm mad at that—"

Ryda placed her hand over my mouth. "Please, shut your corny ass up." She chuckled.

I removed her hand from my mouth then pinned her to the bed by her wrists.

"Shut me up," I told her before kissing her as I positioned myself between her legs.

She wrapped her legs around my waist and her arms around my neck as she gazed deeply into my eyes.

"I love you, Psycho. Please don't ever doubt me again," she said as she gently tugged on my earlobes.

I gave her a soft kiss on the lips before rolling over and pulling her on top of me.

"Baby, you have to understand, life changes for me on a daily. That's the way it's been all my life until I met you. You're the only constant thing I've had in my life, and I can't lose you."

She smiled as she caressed the side of my face then down to my chin. "You won't, but if you keep flipping out on me, I'ma have to chin check your ass." She giggled as she playfully punched me in the chin.

I flipped her onto her back and pushed her knees back. "See, now I gotta show you who wears the pants in this house, Mrs. Jordan."

Ryda looked at me with a scrunched-up face.

"Mrs. Jordan?" she asked with raised brows. "It's Ms. Persons," she continued.

"Yeah, for now. Forever my Ryda?"

She smiled before answering. "Forever your Ryda, Mr. Persons." She chuckled.

"Oh, see, now you got jokes." I laughed as I tickled her unmercifully.

Ryda laughed as she kicked and squirmed, trying to get away from me. I had a strong hold on her, making it impossible for her to free herself. As she continued struggling, she started to turn beet red, and her breathing became heavy as if she were winded.

"You ready to give up?" I asked, chuckling.

"Yes," she replied, trying to recover from laughing so hard.

Grabbing both of her wrist with one hand, I pinned her arms over her head then slowly caressed her body with my other hand. She inhaled then exhaled a deep breath. With my fingertips barely touching her skin, I slid my hand up her thigh until I reached her sweet spot. She slowly licked her lips as I used my thumb to apply pressure to her bud through her panties then moved it in a circular motion.

"Mmm." She moaned softly.

I lifted her shirt and planted a soft moist kiss on her stomach.

"Nope, we are not doing this," she said as she pushed my hand away.

I ignored her as I continued the pattern of lifting her shirt and kissing her body until her nice, plump breasts were exposed. I lifted off her then stared down at her beautiful, exposed body. Ryda was breathing so hard that I could see her stomach sucking inward, as she was anticipating my next move. I licked then sucked my bottom lip into my mouth, biting down to hold it in place. Watching her lying there, squirming and breathing heavily, while I had her restrained put an idea in my head. I flashed her a devilish grin as I let her wrist go then got out the bed.

"Psycho, what are you up to?" she questioned with a puzzle expression as she sat up on the bed.

I laughed a wicked sounding laugh then gave her a wink. "Wait, I'll be back," I said as I hurried out of the bedroom door, ignoring Ryda's questions.

"Psycho, stop playing for real. What are you doing?"

I still didn't answer.

She called out my name a few times, trying to get me to answer her, but I continued to ignore her as I went about the kitchen, collecting the items I needed.

"I know damn well you not in there warming up food!" she shouted from the bedroom when she heard me pressing the buttons on the microwave.

"Just sit tight. I'll be back!" I shouted back to her.

A few minutes later, I returned to the room with my hands behind my back. Ryda's eyes followed me from the door to the dresser to get the incense and incense holder, then over to the table beside the bed.

"Psycho, what the hell—" she started.

I placed my finger over her mouth. "Shhh, relax," I commanded, giving her that devilish grin again before planting a soft kiss on the tip of her nose.

After placing the incense and container that I was holding on the table, I went around the room, closing all the blinds and black-out curtains, trying to get the room as dark as I could. I grabbed the colorful, flameless candle set that Ryda brought off the shelf then placed the candles around the room and turned them on.

"Let me see. Let's go with red," I mumbled to myself as I used the remote to change the color of the candles.

The scent of vanilla filled the air as the glow of red from the candles made the atmosphere in the room appear more romantic. I looked over at Ryda; she was sitting in the middle of the bed with her knees pulled to her chest and a huge grin on her face. She looked up at me wide eyed as she brushed her hair behind her ear.

"Lay down," I commanded, walking over to the table next to the bed.

Keeping up with my love for the music from back in the day, I grabbed my iPod and scrolled to my R&B playlist. As soon as I hit play, R. Kelly's "12 Play" came on. I snickered to myself then bit down on my bottom lip, giving Ryda my sexiest look. She smiled shyly as she gave me the once over. Another thing I loved about fucking older women was that they taught me things—like how to enhance the sex by using your five senses, and I was about to utilize all Ryda's senses to enhance the shit I was about to do to her.

I put a Patchouli incense in the holder. It was one of Ryda's favorite scents. She loved the earthy smell mixed with a hint of sweetness. I read somewhere that its scent was known to awaken sexual energy, and I wanted to find out how true that statement was. I lit the incense and waited until I could smell the scent, then blew the fire out. The sweetness of the vanilla scent added an extra sweetness to the more woody, earthy scent of the Patchouli incense, creating a beautiful fragrance. Ryda closed her eyes and took a whiff of the scent.

"That smells good together," she said, opening her eyes.

I nodded my head in agreement as I used my fingers to close her eyes. Grabbing the container, containing the honey that I warmed up from the table, I dipped my finger in it to make sure it cooled down enough; then, I drizzled the warm honey across her lips, dripping a little into her mouth before kissing her passionately.

"Mmm." She moaned into my mouth as the sweetness of the honey swirled around, toying with our taste buds.

Ryda wrapped her arms around my neck to pull me deeper into the kiss. I shook my head no as I pulled away from her to resist her and break the kiss. Continuing with my plan to explore Ryda's body, I dripped honey down the middle of her chest, around her nipples, and then down her stomach, making a trail of sticky sweetness, leading to the honey pot that she held between her thighs.

RYDA

Psycho had me feeling as if I were about to explode. The things that he began doing with that honey had my box tingling and ready for action. I loved his foreplay, but I was ready for the main event. As he began with the honey from my lips and then commenced to drizzling it down my body until he reached my already throbbing sweet spot, I began to shutter with anticipation. All my life, my body had been a playground for men, but none of them made me want or desire sex like Psycho had; and I never imagined that I could love a man's touch as much.

As soft moans escaped from my mouth, his strong hands maneuvered around my body, and I began to submit. Of course, I was forever his Ryda, but all of that talk about being Mrs. Jordan had me on cloud nine, and as he began to thrust deeply inside of me, I found myself throwing the pussy extra hard at him. My body screamed in pleasure as our connection seemed to deepen with each stoke. I wanted to be his forever and a day, and at that moment, all I could think about was how much I loved this man and what I could do to help make our lives better.I had to. If it were the last thing I did, I'd ride for this man until the wheels fell off.

Lying in bed, recovering from our sexual escapade, my stomach began to growl. I decided to slide from underneath Psycho's arm, grab a long tee and slippers, and then head to the kitchen so I could throw down for my man and myself. One thing about Psycho's ass: he might be knocked out sleep now, but the moment the aroma from my food tickled his nostrils, his ass would come around like a panting dog, begging for food, tongue out and all. I chuckled to myself as the thought of that image ran through my mind. I went into the kitchen and turned on the lights.

"I'm so sick of this shit," I mumbled, scrunching my face as I began stomping, swatting, and hitting wildly at the roaches that seemed to have been magically appearing on the walls, floors, and the counters.

"This is some nasty, fucked up shit," I said under my breath as I began spraying roach spray wildly and watching these nasty muthafuckas fall to their deaths. I needed to talk to Psycho about leaving food out and shit. His ass may as well had left a sign out, saying 'welcome to the roach motel; we leave the light on for you.' I shook my head in disgust, trying my best not to squeal at this nasty shit and wake Psycho up.

After spraying roach spray, I grabbed the bleach and pine sol and began to give the kitchen a good, old fashion cleaning. I hated nasty shit, and seeing those roaches had my mind fucked up, thinking that I would cook some shit, and roaches would appear in my food.

"Ewww!" I hissed in a childlike manner as I frowned my face, shaking that thought out of my mind.

As I got down on my hands and knees, scrubbing the kitchen floor, my mind started drifting back to the Saturday morning cleaning spree Sunny and I used to have. Just like me, she hated filth and would tear the apartment apart, cleaning everything from ceiling fans to the base boards. I missed her. The truth was, she'd been on my mind a lot lately. I began to sing the song "Reach Out, I'll Be There" by The Four

Tops. It was one of Sunny's favorites, and she made sure it was on her playlist as she cleaned the house, singing it loudly.

For some reason, that song made me think about Psycho and myself. I began to think how it would be once we completed a big hit and came into some big money. We would live like some fucking kings and queens, buy shit that niggas could only dream about, and have daily and weekly routines like normal, married couples. We could even finally have some real friends who could be trusted. A mile-wide grin grew on my face just thinking about the life we could have.

A sudden noise at the entrance of the kitchen startled me. I turned my head around to find a drained Psycho leaning against the wall with his arms folded across his chest. Not realizing that I'd spent two hours of detail cleaning this damn kitchen, he stared at me with a confused look.

"What the fuck you smiling for?" he questioned as I began putting away the cleaning supplies and started to gather food to cook for our dinner.

"Nothing. Just thinking about how shit would be once we make a few changes," I retorted as I walked up to him, placing my arms around his neck, and inviting his hands to explore my body as our tongues found and connected with each other as if a magnet were pulling us together.

"Mmmmm." I moaned against his lips, kissing him passionately.

"The good life, huh? That's what you're in here smiling about, Ryda?" Psycho spoke as he pulled away from the kiss, planting a few more quick kisses on my lips.

The question kind of took me by surprise, as Psycho's expression held an intense gaze.

"Baby, I know we are doing all we can in order to survive. You know I'll do—" I began, but he cut me off.

"You not doing that shit no more, Ryda. Fuck that! I'll live with these fucking roaches until my balls grow grey hair before I allow you to sell my pussy for money."

I took in a deep breath, not wanting to snap the fuck out before I spoke. Not caring how I answered, I just simply went for it.

"Psycho, that shit was my past. Do you understand me? My past. I'm not giving my pussy away, and you will have to get over that shit and not continue to bring that up every time the discussion of money comes to table." I snarled as I began to take food out of the refrigerator and freezer, slamming it on the counter as I got ready to prep our food. I was sick of Psycho thinking that I had no other options rather than turning tricks for dick and cash.

"Baby, I'm sorry. I didn't mean to offend you. I was just saying that I didn't want my woman thinking of shit to do to put us in a better situation." His tone had changed.

I eyeballed him suspiciously and continued to pout as I began to chop my onions, bell peppers, mushrooms, and carrots for my chicken breasts that I was about to bake.

"Psycho, I just want you to trust me when I tell you that I'm here for us, and what you do, I got you, and what I do, I need for you to have my back. The Jordans can take over Memphis, or shit, get the fuck out of Memphis and start a new life as we planned. Ain't shit for us here anyway." I smiled as he walked closer to me and put his arms around me from the back and began nibbling on my ear.

"Oh, so you like that name? You wanna be Mrs. Jordan now?" he teased, and my girlish giggle escaped my mouth.

"Well, before we talk about an official name change, I need to figure out our next move."

…

Dinner was ready, and I'd made baked chicken, rice, broccoli with cheese, and garlic bread. Psycho's ass was smashing the food as if it were about to run off his plate. We talked about life and our plans to get out of this apartment and make some serious moves. Psycho wasn't trying to hear me when I told him I had an airtight plan to make sure that we made it out alive, with racks up to our fucking ear, but he had to trust me if he really wanted to go after the bag.

"Ryda, we not robbing a fucking bank, so cut that shit out. We ain't that damn good yet!" he shouted through the bathroom door.

Knowing that he couldn't see me, I frowned my face and stuck my tongue out at him.

"I'm about to go on a mission. Scope out our next lick so we can get this money. We need to make some moves," he spoke as he appeared from the bathroom in all black, looking sexy as fuck. I hopped out of bed, turning off the TV, and began to scurry around the room, grabbing my all black.

"What the fuck are you doing?" he questioned as if he forgot we were in this shit together.

"What do you mean *what the fuck am I doing*? You just said you needed to make some moves. If you're going out to find a target or to get a quick lick, I'm riding with you. I'm yo' Ryda; remember?" I huffed.

"Nah, I don't need yo' ass fucking shit up," he spat, and I got mad.

"Fucking shit up?" I looked at him as if he had lost his mind. "You the one that fucked shit up," I continued, reminding him that he was the reason why we were in this shit now, and that he was the one that just fucked shit up.

Running to the closet, I pulled out an old, oversized purse and tossed a few racks on the bed.

"When I was told to save for a rainy day, I anticipated every thunderstorm, tornado, and drought. Yeah, we're running low, but just like you got me, I got you."

His mouth hung open as he brought his attention towards me.

"So this is where we are, Ryda? We hiding money from each other? What? You out here shaking ass when I'm sleep? You out here tricking again? Where the fuck did you get this money? Cutty said you were out here on some hoe shit, and I should have listened."

I looked at him with confusion on my face. "First, this is my last fucking time telling you, I'm done with that, and I'm not fucking no other man—not for money or anything else. I don't want any other man but you. Get that through that thick ass skull of yours because I'm not ever having this fucking conversation again."

"You expect me to believe that when you been moving funny, leaving the house and coming back with money, and not saying shit to me. I'm sorry, Ryda, but shit don't work that way."

Without responding to his stupid ass accusation, I stormed to the closet and grabbed the small purse off the hook then stormed back to the room and dumped its contents on the bed.

"I sold some of the jewelry I accumulated working for Panama, so that *we* could have money to do what we had to do, and so—"

"So you could get the fuck away from me?" he inquired.

"Yeah, Psycho, so I could get the fuck away from you," I replied in a serious tone.

"So again, Cutty was right," he stated.

"What the fuck do Cutty have to do with this, and why in the hell is he speaking about me like he fucking know me? I was leaving your ass because you were tripping. Do you not remember that? Fuck you mean *Cutty was right*? Fuck a damn Cutty."

"He said some things that made some sense at the time. I thought it was bull shit. But now—" he started, but I was too pissed to let him finish.

"But now, shit! That nigga don't know me! You do. What I don't understand is, how in the hell did you let this nigga get in your head? He ain't shit but a plug. Why in the fuck do he feel as if he could speak on me to you?"

"Ryda, calm down. He wasn't talking about you like you think. We was talking about them niggas running up in our shit, and we was trying to piece shit to—"

Psycho paused as if a light bulb just flicked on in his head, and the look on his face turned into a scowl.

"What's up, Psycho? What's wrong?" I questioned confused as I took his hand and sat on the bed.

I couldn't believe the shit Psycho was telling me. Cutty accusing me of setting Psycho up was enough to anger me, but to hear that he was involved in nigga's robbing us had my blood boiling.

"That snake ass, dirty ass, bitch ass nigga. He tried it! Muthafucka wanted to point fingers at me so his grimy ass won't get found out. I got something for his ass. Yeah, we gonna get his ass. He got to die. Ain't no ifs, ands, buts, or supposes about it."

Psycho agreed as we sat on the bed, discussing different ways to carry out our plan. I didn't know Cutty at all, so I had to rely on the information that Psycho was giving me to come up with something. After getting the information needed, I finally came up with the perfect plan.

"Ryda, Cutty is smart, and I don't think that shit will work. He'll catch on real quick."

"Not if we follow my plan." I placed his face in my hands. "Look, Psycho, this is gonna involve me getting into full character. I have to become Innocence, but this not gonna work unless you trust me to lead. Psycho, I need to know that you can do that. Do you trust me?"

Looking deep into my eyes, Psycho nodded his head. "Yeah, Ryda, I trust you," he replied in a serious tone.

"Good, because we gonna need help, and I know exactly who I can go to." I quickly slipped on my shoes. "Give me the keys. I'm driving," I added as I held my hand out.

Psycho looked at me with raised brows as if he were wondering what I was up to. I tilted my head slightly to the right as I pursed my lips and raised my brows with a look that let him know that I was dead ass.

"We don't have a car, crazy," he reminded me, chuckling.

It had completely slipped my mind that Psycho had gotten rid of the car. I flopped down on the bed and let out a frustrated sigh.

"Don't worry. I'ma holler at Bruce tomorrow. I'm sure he will get us another one," he stated as he placed his arm around my neck and kissed me on the temple, trying to calm me.

I was highly upset and disappointed. I was ready to put my plan into motion. Cutty crossed me, but worse than that, he'd crossed Psycho. There was no way in hell I could let him live after that.

PSYCHO

Ryda's ass had gone from zero to a hundred in a matter of seconds. You could tell that my baby's mind was all over the place. Her crazy ass was asking me for keys to a car that we didn't have, had me looking at her like, *what the fuck is she really planning?*

I laid on the bed with my arms behind my head and my fingers clasped together, thinking while looking up at the ceiling.

"Baby, what are you thinking about? You do trust me, right?" Ryda questioned as I turned my head to face her while staring into her beautiful eyes.

"I trust you. You're forever my Ryda, right?" I countered as she laid next to me and began to nestle her body into mine.

"No matter what happens, Psycho, I'll always be your Ryda."

The tone that she used sent this eerie feeling over me, as I began to think that something was not going to go according to her plan. Shaking off those thoughts and wanting to shed light on this intense mood we both seemed to be in, I pulled her in, kissed the top of her forehead, and spoke.

"Ryda, I've never allowed a woman, or anyone for that matter, to have full control over anything I did. Not even that bitch of a mother, so the fact that I'm willing to put my trust in you, should really tell you something," I offered, and she sat up and looked me in the eyes.

"Ryda, I've never loved anyone as much as I'm loving you. I've already trusted you with my heart, so now, I'm trusting you with my life. Please don't fuck this up, baby girl. If you really don't have this shit, it's cool. I'll always have us. You don't have to pretend to show me that you are down for a nigga," I sincerely spoke, meaning every word.

"Psycho, baby, I love you, but most importantly, I love *us*. You and me; me and you. No matter what, I would never put us in a position that would cause us to be away from each other forever, or even for an extended period of time. Trust me, baby. I got this, and Cutty will pay. Let's get some rest so we can get up early and meet up with Bruce. It's go time," she affirmed, and I couldn't help but smile. Ryda was amazing, and I was lucky enough to bump into her crazy ass that night in the alley.

…

Waking up feeling refreshed, I noticed Ryda's ass curled up under the cover while soft moans of 'Psycho' escaped from her lips. I smiled, knowing she was dreaming about me tearing that pussy up, but it was time to make moves, and I needed to make them now so we could get to whatever plans Ryda had. I knew her ass was gonna be pissed when she woke up. She wanted to roll out with me, but I could move and shake faster on the solo tip, and she would have to find a way to understand.

I grabbed the money that Ryda had taken out that old beat up purse she kept in the closet and shook my head.

Women always have a nest some damn where for a rainy day, I thought as I kissed her head, knowing that I had enough money to make a couple of moves and come back and listen to this damn plan.

Ipulled the covers up over her, just the way she liked it, and scribbled a note on the sticky pad that simply stated that I went for a walk then got the fuck low.

Bruce's shop was a few miles down the road, and my only options were to either walk or catch the bus. And I ain't never been the nigga to use public transportation. There were too many ignorant ass muthafuckas riding that shit, and I could always see a nigga trying to flex and my ass stomping him out and possibly going to jail. Fuck that shit, I'd rather die before I went down. Exhaling the breath that I took in, I put my hands in my pockets and made the almost three-mile hike to Bruce's shop, and just as I thought, the nigga came through for me on the wheels.

As I was admiring the work Bruce and his crew did on the car, he asked if he could holler at me about something.

"Come on, Bruce. You like an old ass uncle or something. You can talk to me about anything; all you have to do is open yo' mouth."

Bruce shook his head and let out a slight chuckle. "Boy, if you ain't J.B all over again," he commented as he sat on top of a car that he was working on and began speaking.

"You know me and your daddy went way back since we were youths, and I loved him like he was my own blood, and I feel the same about you."

"Yeah, Bruce, I know, and I look at you like family as well." I eyed him suspiciously, trying to figure out why we were having this conversation again.

"And you know that I'll protect you like one of my own, and some of the shit I'm hearing, I'm not liking—like niggas running up in your shit. Why didn't you come holler at me about that?"

"No need to worry, old man. I got shit handled," I stated matter-of-factly.

"Yajir, take heed to what I'm about to say. These niggas out here claiming to be your friends." He shook his head. "They not your friends. You hear what I'm saying?"

Bruce was a business man, but he was also a street nigga, and when shit wasn't moving right, he was quick to call that shit out. Reading between the lines, I already knew what Bruce was telling me. The only nigga out here that Bruce knew as my friend was Cutty. My chest got tight as anger shot through my body. Knowing a nigga that I knew for so fucking long had something to do with that shit was already fucking with me. Now, thinking that the nigga was out here bragging on the shit like I was a bitch made nigga had me thinking all types of shit.

What's really good, Cutty? You trying to put shit out in the streets to see if I got balls enough to step to you? Those were just some of the questions that were going through my mind. What Cutty didn't know was I had balls bigger than got damn Texas, and he shouldn't have ever crossed me.

"What you hear, Bruce?" I inquired, giving him my full attention.

"I might be an old man, but with age comes wisdom. One thing I learned all my years in the streets running with your daddy: no matter how old you get, always keep your eyes and ears on them muthafuckas. When I hear that a nigga spitting fire on my fam, I don't sit around listening and chucking and shit. I'm not the nigga that take the shit lightly, you understand? If that nigga Cutty and his niggas gunning for you, don't hesitate to ask. I'm here for you. I'll set this whole damn city on fire. You J. B.'s son; ain't no nigga gonna fuck with you in these streets and not pay with their life," Bruce spoke, and that confirmed all my thoughts. Bruce was never a nigga to spit fire on the next nigga's shit, but he always spoke the truth.

He hopped off the car and gave me dap, and then he handed me the keys to the car that he was giving me.

"Don't worry about this shit. Niggas ain't checking for no damn Toyota Corolla. We chopped this shit and rebuilt this fucker to last. You know you drive the fuck outta a Toyota, so you good to go. Just be safe and remember what I said. Watch who the fuck you call your friend, and don't hesitate to call."

"Bruce, man, thanks for the wheels. You sure I can't give you anything for this shit?" I questioned.

He blankly stared at me, letting me know that I already knew the answer to my own damn question.

The Corolla wasn't flashy, but it was nice, clean, and purred like a kitten. Bruce might not have thought this was shit, but this was everything to me, and when shit got in order for me, I was going to make sure I looked out for Bruce. I nodded towards him to assure him that I was understanding the shit he was spitting. After dapping him up again, I took the keys and slid into my new whip.

"Ryda is going to love this shit." I smiled, talking out loud, not realizing I spoke my thoughts.

"You really feeling yo' girl, huh, Yajir?" Bruce inquired, and I hesitated with my reply.

Not answering his question, I simply smiled before speaking. "Thanks, Bruce. You really came through for a nigga, and I got you after I take care of my business."

I knew Bruce wasn't about to take money from me willingly. I offered a few times during our conversation. As I backed out of his shop, I tossed five K at his feet, in a rubber band. He picked it up, smiled, and shook his head as he pushed the button for the garage door to open, and I peeled away.

Five K wasn't shit, and this whip was worth way more, but I had to give his ass something, I guess you can call it a man thing because I'd be damned if I ever felt like a nigga gave me anything.

On the ride back to our spot, Ryda began calling my phone. Cursing myself for taking longer than I wanted to, I reluctantly picked up the phone.

"Yes, baby?" I answered.

"Where the fuck you at? You ain't go for a walk that fucking long. Don't play these games with me, Psycho. If I did some shit like that to you, you'll be turning over every fucking brick in Memphis looking for my ass," she ranted as I held the phone away from my ear.

"Ryda, calm down. I just went to see Bruce. I got a us a ride. Now I'm gonna go to the grocery store. I'll be home in a lil' while."

"Why you ain't take me, huh? You knew I would want to go with you, so why didn't you wake me?"

"Look, we can talk when I get home. I'm driving, and I don't need this shit right now," I replied in an annoyed tone.

Ryda responded by hanging up on me. I wiped my eyes and pinched the bridge of my nose as I sat at the red light. I was getting sick of all this back and forth and the petty little arguments that Ryda and I had. I'd never been one to do too much bickering and shit. That was part of the reason why I stayed to myself. I didn't have time for the dumb shit people do.

After grabbing food from the grocery store, I headed home, hoping that Ryda would have calmed down by the time I got there. Once I entered the house, all hope was gone.

"See, Psycho, this the same shit you did when we was in the hotel. I don't like to be cooped up in the fucking house all damn day," Ryda fussed as I placed the grocery bags on the table.

I didn't even get in the house good, and she had already started running her damn mouth. I wasn't in the mood for this shit.

"Ryda, I told you that I had to go see Bruce to get us a car," I reiterated as I grabbed a beer out of the fridge.

I knew it was too damn early to be drinking, but the shit Bruce told me was weighing heavy on my mind. *Watch who the fuck you call your friend* was boggling the shit out of me since I really didn't call nobody my friend, and the only nigga I had around Bruce was Cutty, so it had to be him that he was talking about. That shit was fucking with my mental. Cutty was capable of a lot of shit, but I wasn't tripping off that shit, though, 'cause he didn't know what the fuck I was capable of. My only concern was, why? Why the fuck was this nigga fucking with me? I ain't never did shit to him. I even stopped hitting dope boys and started hitting stores instead 'cause this nigga was taking over territories, and I didn't want to step on his toes.

"So what? You was just gonna cut me out of the plan or something? You knew I wanted to go with you, but you dipped out, off the early morning, while I was sleep, on some sneaky-type shit. What? You on a solo mission now?" Ryda continued fussing, placing her hands on her hips as she gave me a questioning look.

"Ryda, look. I'm not tryna beef right now. Chill for a minute."

I popped the top off my beer and chugged it down in one big gulp. I threw the empty bottle in the trash then grabbed another one out of the fridge. I popped the top and sat at the table and started rubbing my temples. Ryda was starting to give me a fucking headache.

"Instead of downing those fucking beers like you a got damn drunk, you need to stop procrastinating on this fucking plan. We need to be putting shit in motion. Ain't nobody got time to be dragging ass while Cutty out there thinking shit sweet," she ranted, tossing the items she needed to cook breakfast on the counter.

"Ryda, look. Just take a minute to breath. Shit, calm down," I said, taking another gulp of my Heineken.

She whipped her head around so fast, I thought her head was about to fly off.

"Calm down? *Calm down?* Why, Psycho? 'Cause it's your boy? I don't give a fuck who he is; Cutty's gonna get what's coming to him. What the fuck I don't understand is why the hell you not as pissed off as me. That's *your* muthafuckin' nigga. You went running *your* muthafuckin' mouth to him, giving him all the fucking ammunition he needed to run up in your shit, and you telling me to calm the fuck down. Nigga, you need to—"

"Shut the fuck up, Lanae! Damn!" I yelled, jumping up and slamming my fist on the table.

Ryda was looking at me like I was crazy. She knew I was mad as hell, but she still didn't back down.

"Lanae?" She chuckled in anger. "So you calling me by my born name? That's supposed to do what? Shut me up? That ain't happening. I told your ass not to talk to me like that and—"

"And if you didn't run yo' got damn mouth so fucking much, then I wouldn't have to. I mean damn, Ryda! You always poppin' off. Calm the fuck down sometimes. Everything don't require all that shit." I gave her an evil look as I went to the fridge and grabbed another bottle of beer then went to the bedroom.

As the loud sounds of Ryda slamming the cabinet doors and banging pots and pans filled the apartment, I shook my head. I placed the other bottle of beer on the table beside the bed, then grabbed my Beats and my iPod, scrolled to my gansta rap playlist, and pressed play. The intro to

Scarface's "I Seen a Man Die" started, I sat back with my back against the headboard with one leg stretched on the bed, took a sip of my beer, and then closed my eyes, trying to relax my mind.

I got my love for old school music from my father. I remember him always bumping music in the house, and I would sit there watching him—singing or rapping the lyrics, bobbing his head as he moved about, doing whatever he was doing at the time. That was my only connection to him now; listening to the music that he loved always put me in a chilled mood.

Right before the song ended, I felt a presence in the room. I opened my eyes to find Ryda leaning against the door frame with her arms crossed, staring at me with furrowed brows. I hit pause on my iPod and removed my head phones.

"Ryda, look. I'm really—" I started.

She put her hand up, stopping me from continuing to speak. She walked over to the bed, so I moved my leg so she could sit down.

"I'm sorry, Psycho. I shouldn't have fussed at you like that. I just want you to understand my frustrations." The apologetic look in her eyes let me know that she was speaking truthfully and from the heart. "I know I fly off the handle, and sometimes, that makes me not think things through. I should have taken heed to your mood and gave you your space. I apologize for that," she continued.

I stroked her hair then pulled her in for a quick kiss on her lips. "I understand yo' frustrations, but you need to understand mine, too. You think any of this shit is easy for me? I'm used to handling shit on my own, not caring about nothing or nobody but my damn self. Now, I got you to worry about. I can't let nothing happen to you. I will never forgive myself."

"Nothing is going to happen to me, Psycho. I'm not going nowhere; you understand? I'm riding with you no matter what. I got your back just like you got mine. Besides that, I can't live without you anyway, so I might as well ride."

She playfully mushed my head then flashed me a huge grin. I pulled her closer to me then kissed her passionately as I pulled her on top of me, gripping her ass. She pulled herself off me.

"Talk to me. What got you in this fucked up ass mood?" she asked as she sat back in the same spot she was before and started rubbing the bottom of my leg.

I really didn't want to tell her what Bruce had said, 'cause I didn't want her to get pissed off again. At the same time, I knew that if I didn't tell her, she wasn't gonna let the shit go, and that would only have irritated the fuck out of me. I laid my back against the headboard and let out a sigh as I ran my hands down my face.

"Bruce told me some shit that's weighing heavy on my mind," I told her as I grabbed my beer off the table and took a drink.

"What he tell you?" she asked in a concerned tone.

Just as I thought, once I told her what Bruce had said, she went off. She hopped off the bed quick then started pacing back and forth, clapping her hands together, ranting. I didn't know what the hell she was saying, but she was annoying the hell out of me, and I had to tune her out before I snapped. I ran my hand across my forehead as I inhaled and exhaled deeply.

"Psycho, you hear what I'm saying? Cutty is your man," she fumed.

"Stop saying that shit, Ryda. He's not my man. Yes, our mothers are friends, and we was around each other a lot, but we ain't like that. We did some shit together growing up, I buy my tree from the nigga, and we kick it sometimes, but that's as far as we go," I explained.

"Well, whatever it is, he knows you, and he's running around here plotting against you. That's some bullshit, and he needs to be handled *asap*. Maybe you in your feelings or something. Is that why you ain't mad for real for real?"

I didn't even bother with responding to the bullshit she was talking. I popped the top off my third beer and proceeded to drink my shit.

Ryda stood silent with her arms folded across her chest, mugging me, as her eyes stayed glued on me.

"You got a car. Now give me the keys. I need to go holler at somebody so I can get this shit started," she said in a calm voice.

"No the fuck you not. It can wait. You need to understand something. I might have given you the lead on this plan, but I'm the fucking head nigga in charge. This my shit, and we move when I say move. You ain't from these streets, and you don't know these niggas. I do. I know you have a plan, and I'm good on that, but right now, you have no choice but to follow my fucking orders. Now, sit your ass down somewhere, and calm the hell down. 'Fore I give you a real reason to be hollering and screaming."

My little sex reference had Ryda leaning against the dresser, twirling her hair with her finger, blushing. I shook my head.

"I swear, the only time you stop running yo' mouth is when I slide dick up in you."

Her face started turning bright red.

"Is that what you want, Ryda? You want me to slide this dick up in you? You want that act right?" I questioned as she tried hard to hide the smile that was threatening to spread across her face as I walked towards to her.

Using my body to pin her against the dresser, I leaned down so that I was so close to her that she could feel my breath against her lips. She slowly licked her lips to moisten them as she prepared for the kiss she so desperately wanted.

"Not gon' happen," I stated as I quickly licked her lip then backed up off her.

She pushed me away. "Nobody want your lil' dry ass dick anyway," she lied.

"I bet if I pulled this big muthafucka out, yo' lil' ass won't waste no time wetting the muthafucka up with that big ass mouth of yours." I chuckled.

She rolled her eyes. "Get the hell away from me, pussy breath ass nigga," she said as she pushed past me.

I shook my head laughing at her little attitude as I headed to the kitchen. I grabbed my White Owls off the table; then I reached in the cabinet, got a glass, and rinsed and filled it with water. I took the glass of water in the bedroom and handed it to Ryda.

"What's that for?" she asked, looking baffled.

"You real thirsty right now. I thought you needed it," I replied nonchalantly as I shrugged my shoulders.

Ryda gave me the evil eye then slapped the glass out of my hand and onto the floor. I shrugged my shoulders again.

"Well, go take a cold shower, and maybe if you act like you got some sense, I'll crack yo' back in the morning—give you a lil' wake up and get yo' mind right dick." I blew her a kiss then commenced to rolling a blunt.

"Ryda, look. Like I said, I'm down with your plan and anything you feel we need to do. I trust you. I just need you to understand that you can't just jump when you in your feelings. That's how you make mistakes. Like honestly, I wasn't thinking when I came in the check cashing place, I was acting on my emotions, but you was there to do what we needed to do to get us out of there before the cops came."

"Yeah, but barely, though," she replied.

"It don't matter. Had I been level headed, I wouldn't have come in there like that. All I'm saying is we need to find a place then figure out the plan. We gotta plan that shit carefully. Fucking with Cutty, there's no room for error. That nigga don't give a fuck about nobody for real. Niggas get that shit twisted with him all the time. They think that because they work for him, they cool, and he cares about them. In his mind, everybody is expendable. If it don't benefit him, it don't matter."

"How does running up in our house benefit him? What do we have to do with his shit?" she questioned, trying to make sense of this entire situation.

"Man, Cutty been on some dumb shit with me since we was kids. He always in some kind of self-created competition with me. I don't know why. It wasn't like either one of us had shit. We both started doing shit so that we could get shit. Like this one time, we both was pressed for the Jordan Spiz'ikes, the white, varsity red, and true blue ones. We cut grass, swept the floor in the barber shop, and everything to get them bitches. I was grinding, while he procrastinated, and I got mine first. This nigga was pissed. Then, the very next day, this nigga popped up over my house on some goofy as shit, acting like he came to chill with me and shit. He started pressing me out to try the shoes on. I let him, and he started flexin', thinking he looked fly. This nigga tried to keep me distracted, thinking I was gonna forget he had my shoes on so he could take them bitches."

"That's crazy," Ryda replied, shaking her head.

"Yeah, that's how that nigga is. He don't like for nobody to have something he don't. I knew right then and there that I couldn't fuck with Cutty like that. I keep shit on a certain level with him." I took a puff of my blunt then blew the smoke in the air.

"I'm telling you, baby. Cutty ain't the type of nigga you can just run up on. He's too smart for that. Just like I know he slipped up, he knows he did. Now, I don't know if this nigga gunning for me or talking reckless out the mouth, trying to see where my head is at. Either way, we got to get the fuck outta this apartment as soon as possible."

"Ok, Psycho, I'll follow your lead. We can relax today so you can get your mind right, but tomorrow, we got to make moves. I know just the person to go see," she stated as she headed to the kitchen to finish cooking.

RYDA

Trying to shield myself from the sunlight that beamed through the window, I threw the pillow over my head. It seemed that it was no escape. As I stretched and yawned, Psycho pulled me closer to him, wrapping his arms around me.

"You ready for your reminder to behave today?" he asked, planting moist kisses on the nape of my neck and then on my shoulder.

I turned around and cupped his face in my hands.

"You can remind me, but I can't promise that I'll behave." I gave him a soft kiss on his bottom lip before sucking it into my mouth.

"I actually feel like being bad now. Very bad," I stated before kissing him passionately then disappearing under the cover.

After spending another hour in bed, I was ready to start the day.

"Okay, Psycho, get up. We ain't got time to be laying around all day, being lazy. We got moves to make, and I got to go see somebody a little later," I told him as I gathered my things for a shower.

Psycho pulled the cover over his head as he turned to the side, not paying me any attention. I hated when people ignored me when I was saying something that was important to me. I grabbed the deodorant off the dresser and threw it at him.

"Get the hell up!" I shouted.

"Woman, have you lost yo' got damn mind?" he barked as he hopped out of bed, rubbing the spot on his head where the deodorant hit him.

"I see you got up." I chuckled as I turned to go into the bathroom.

Before I could take another step, Psycho snatched me by the arm and jacked me up against the wall.

"Let's get this shit straight right the fuck now. I've let you get away with too much shit, but you're pressing yo' luck. You will not put yo' hands on me, throw shit at me, or try to kick me no more. I'm not built for that shit, and I'm gon' end up fuckin' yo' lil ass up." His gaze was intense as he spoke through clenched teeth.

I opened my mouth, getting ready to say some slick shit out of the mouth; but before I could utter a word, Psycho covered my mouth with his hand.

"Don't even throw that fucking threat about taking my life, as you know I don't give a fuck about yo' threat. Now what's gon' happen is, I'ma let you go, you not gon' retaliate, and you gon' take yo' ass in the bathroom and wash yo' funky ass. You got me?" he spoke in an authoritative voice as he looked at me with raised brows.

My heart was beating a mile a minute as I stared into Psycho's eyes. I didn't know if I should be afraid or turned on. Either way, I fell in love with Psycho all over again. I nodded my head in agreement.

"Good. Now that that's settled, when you get dressed, we can have breakfast and discuss your plan," he stated as I wrapped my arms around his neck.

I tried to pull him in for a kiss, but he resisted, and I wasn't strong enough to force the kiss.

"Don't try that shit. We ain't doing nothing but what I just said. Now go," he commanded, pointing at the bathroom.

"Yes, daddy," I teased as I batted my eyes.

"Yeah, don't make me put you over my knee," he joked as he slapped my ass.

"I might like that," I flirted as I turned on my heels and headed to the bathroom to take a shower.

When I got out of the shower, Psycho was in the kitchen, fixing our plates. He cooked sausage, eggs, grits, and toast. I sat down at the table as he placed my plate in down in front of me.

"Thank you, baby," I said as he sat down with his plate.

After saying grace, we proceeded to eat our breakfast and discuss our plan. I was glad that Psycho told me what Bruce said and explained his friendship with Cutty to me. Now I know that he wasn't in his feelings about taking this nigga out. Knowing the shit Psycho revealed to me in further conversation, I was able to come up with a new plan—one that Cutty would never see coming.

Pulling up to The House of Angels, my stomach was in knots. I hadn't stepped foot in this place since the night I killed Panama, and although my former client informed me of who was running the place, I still didn't know what to expect.

"You good?" Psycho asked as he kissed the back of my hand.

"Yeah, I'm good. I'm just not too sure how this shit gonna play out. I haven't spoken to anybody since the day I left, and I'm not sure if I'm still welcomed here," I explained.

Psycho shut the engine off then turned towards me.

"No matter what pops off in here, I got you. Don't worry about shit, aight?" he assured as he stroked then kissed my cheek.

I nodded my head in agreement, and then, he proceeded to open his car door. He walked over to the passenger side and opened the door then held his hand out for me to take. I took his hand, and he helped me out of the car.

"Yo, I got you, aight?" he reiterated. "Forever my Ryda?" he asked as he lifted my chin.

"Forever your Ryda," I replied with a huge smile.

Psycho leaned down and planted a soft kiss on my lips. "Let's do this," I said as he took my hand and led me into the house.

As soon as I walked through the door, Jaquay squealed as she rushed over to me and embraced me tightly.

"Girl, where the hell have you been, and why in the hell you didn't call me to let me know that you were okay?" she questioned as she continued squeezing me to death.

Before I could answer, she looked Psycho up and down then pushed me to the side.

"Who is this fine piece of man candy?" she asked as she gave him the once over again.

"That's my man," I replied, wrapping my arm around Psycho's arm.

Jaquay extended her hand for Psycho to take as she introduced herself.

"I'm Jaquay, and you are?" she introduced in a sing song voice.

Psycho chuckled a little before answering. "Psycho," he answered as he took her hand and kissed the back of it.

I gave him a quick death stare, and he quickly released Jaquay's hand then kissed my cheek.

"Don't get jealous, Innocence. I don't want yo' man even though he's fine as hell," Jaquay teased as she winked at him then sashayed her black ass back over to the desk.

Jaquay had smooth, ebony skin that was bump and blemish free. Her hair was naturally straight and cut into a bob that stopped at her chin. She was beautiful, and even though she was well into her forties, she looked as if she were in her late twenties or early thirties.

"Is she here?" I asked.

Jaquay gave me a questionable look. "Please tell me you not thinking about coming back to this place."

"She's never coming back, and her name is not Innocence," Psycho replied, answering for me.

Jaquay smiled then winked at him again. "I like him, Lanae." She blushed. "She's in the office. Go 'head in there," she added, pointing down the hall.

As we stepped out of the front area into the main area, where the women entertained their clients before heading to their rooms, a few girls came over to me, giving me hugs. I could tell that Psycho was a little uncomfortable, so I cut my conversations short and made my way down the long hallway.

"This the type of shit you use to do?" Psycho asked, referencing how the women were walking around in lingerie and the men was all over them.

"Yes, Psycho. It was my job," I answered truthfully.

As we proceeded up the steps, Allen, one of my former regular clients, was coming down the steps with Candy, one of the girls in the house.

"Innocence, you back working?" he asked excitedly.

Candy rolled her eyes at the excitement in his tone.

"Hell no, she ain't back working. Now move around," Psycho spoke in a threatening tone as he eyeballed the nigga.

Candy chuckled under her breath as she rocked from side to side, gazing at Psycho with a look of lust. But he wasn't paying her no attention. His eyes were still stuck on Allen. I, on the other hand, was starting to get pissed. My breathing started to become rapid, and my body was getting hot as I stared at Candy with anger in my eyes. I hated Candy's low-key hating ass, but I tried to be respectful in Panama's house. But he ain't here now, and if this bitch didn't stop eye fucking my man, I was gonna mop the steps with her blood.

"Can I help you, Candy?" I inquired in a sarcastic tone, taking her attention away from my man.

The bitch was about to come out of me, and I was about two seconds away from going the fuck off on her.

"No, I'm good," she replied, rolling her eyes as she grabbed Allen's arm and continued down the steps.

I continued to mug Candy as she and Allen walked down the steps and disappeared down the hallway.

"Your jealousy is showing," Psycho whispered in my ear.

"Yours too," I replied as we proceeded up the step and down the second, long hallway.

We reached the huge set of double doors, and my stomach started quivering again. I took a deep breath, trying to calm my nerves. Psycho squeezed my hand then kissed the top of my head.

"I'm right beside you," he assured.

I took another deep breath then knocked on the door.

"Come in," the loud but sweet sounding voice called out from the other side of the door.

With trembling hands, I reached for the knob and turned it, slowly opening the door.

"Well, look what the got damn cat done dragged in." Sunny chuckled as she hurried from behind the desk with outstretched arms.

The huge smile on her face let me know that everything was cool, which put my mind and stomach at ease. I let go of Psycho's hands and rushed into her welcoming embrace.

Words could not express how much I'd missed Sunny. I wanted to reach out to her so many times, but I was too afraid of her finding out the truth behind Panama's death. She was so close to him, and I was unsure of how she would feel about me if she knew what I'd done. When my former client from the check cashing place told me that she was running the house, I thought that it was fitting for her. She knew the ins and outs of Panama's operation, and she was the only person that Panama would've trusted to be his successor. And I thought that maybe it was ok for me to reach out to her. Maybe she would understand why I did what I did.

"Girl, where have you been?" she asked as tears filled both our eyes.

I was so overwhelmed with emotion that I couldn't even speak. She was so happy to see me, and at that moment, I knew that I'd made the right choice. Sunny pulled back from the hug, giving me the once over.

"Look at you, looking all good." She took my hand, spun me around, and then pulled me back in for an embrace, squeezing me and rocking from side to side.

After hugging and shedding tears for what seemed like an eternity, Sunny finally let me go.

"Sit down so we can talk," she said dragging me over to her desk.

Then, she noticed Psycho and paused, clutching her chest and staring at Psycho as if she had seen a ghost.

"Oh, I'm sorry, Sunny. I forgot to introduce you two," I said, grabbing Psycho's hand.

"Psycho, this is Sunny. Sunny, this is my boyfriend, Psycho," I introduced.

"Nice to meet you, Sunny," Psycho chirped as he extended his hand for a shake.

Sunny stood frozen with her hands covering her mouth.

"Sunny, are you alright?" I asked with concern in my tone.

She didn't respond; she just stood there, shaking her head back and forth and staring at Psycho with wide eyes.

Psycho was baffled, but I couldn't blame him. I was just as confused as he was. As a lone tear fell from Sunny's eyes, she began to speak in a tremulous voice.

"It can't be. It just can't be," she spoke in a low voice.

She took in a deep breath as if she were trying to fight back her tears then took Psycho's hand and placed it on her chest as she reached out with trembling hands, slowly touching his face.

"Aye, Ryda, I ain't feeling this shit. Get yo' peoples," Psycho said as he leaned away, looking at Sunny as if she were insane.

"Sunny, what's going on?" I asked as I pulled her hand away from Psycho's face.

She snatched her hand away from me and continued to reach for Psycho again.

"Ryda, on some real shit, this ain't cool. I ain't about to be nobody's boy toy," he stressed moving Sunny's hand from his face.

I was staring at the whole scene in disbelief. It was like Sunny was having a mental breakdown or something. She was crying, clutching her chest like she was clutching her pearls, and hyperventilating. I'd never seen her like that before, and I was starting to get worried.

"That face. That voice. I'll never forget," Sunny spoke in a brittle voice, shaking her head as tears poured out of her eyes. "No, it can't be. It just can't be."

SUNNY

I noticed the resemblance as soon as he walked through the door, but I thought that I was only imagining what I was seeing. I tried to ignore it and keep my focus on Lanae, but that face, those eyes, and those lips—I could never forget. And when he spoke, his voice brought a flood of emotions to surface, and I couldn't ignore them any longer. It was as if I had traveled back in time to the day I lost the love of my life.

"Baby, I only want what's best for us. Can't you see it ain't shit but trouble out here in these streets? Look what just happened. You could have been killed," I pleaded with J.B.

"Stephanie, I can't do that. I got too much shit to handle. I get new responsibilities every day," he replied as he grabbed a beer out of the refrigerator and gulped it down.

"What responsibilities, J.B.? You know I'm here for you, and I'm willing to do whatever I can to make sure we are alright. I love you, Jonas Butler. Do you get that?"

I knelt in front of him, looking deeply into his eyes. He placed his beer on the table then cupped my face in his hands. He kissed the top of my forehead.

"I never intended for any of this to happen. When I saw you sitting on the ground, crying, all I wanted to do was to help you," he spoke in a soft tone.

"I know, and I'm so grateful for that. Without you, I don't know where I would have been." I sniffed as a lump formed in my throat.

"Don't think about that, Steph. You didn't deserve to be abused by your uncle. You lost your parents. Your grandmother and aunts should have protected you instead of allowing it to go on." He gave me another long kiss on my forehead.

"I love you, Stephanie, but I'm sorry. I can't give up my lifestyle for you. Not now. Not ever."

The somber tone in his voice made my heart ache, and I began to feel nervous. Something was troubling him, and for some reason, I was afraid to find out. J.B. lifted me off the ground and onto his lap.

"If I could, I would make you my wife right now," he stated, stroking my cheek as tears began to form in his eyes.

"Baby, what's wrong?" I asked in a concerned tone as I wiped away the tear that had now fallen from his eye.

He flashed me a weak smile before kissing me passionately. Without breaking the kiss, I maneuvered around on his lap until I was straddling him.

"I love you so much, Stephanie." He moaned into my mouth as he held me tighter.

"I love you to, Jonas," I replied, still kissing him.

My heart was pounding at the same rhythm as the throbbing pain in my chest. It was as if this were our last kiss. I didn't want it to end. J.B pulled away from the kiss and placed his forehead on top of mine.

"I don't want to lose you," he whispered.

"You're not," I avowed as I ran my hand up his chest and started unbuttoning his shirt.

"No, Stephanie. Stop." He grabbed my hand, pulling it away from his chest.

I knew right then and there that something was wrong, and whatever it was, was gonna tear us apart. One thing that never happened was J.B. resisting sex. I tried to ignore what my heart was telling me. I held him tightly as I kissed the spot on the middle of his neck that drove him crazy.

"This is the hardest thing I ever had to do," he stated in a low tone.

Still trying to ignore the pain in my heart, I continued kissing his neck and trying to unbutton his shirt.

"Stephanie, stop. I have to tell you something."

I acted like I didn't hear him and continued trying to tempt him.

"Stephanie, stop it!" he shouted as he yanked me away from him.

Tears started forming in my eyes. I had no idea what he had to tell me, but something in my heart didn't want me to hear whatever it was that he was about to say.

"Sharie's pregnant," he blurted out.

My heart dropped, and my breathing stopped. I couldn't believe what I was hearing. Out of all the things he could have told me, why did it have to be that? Why did that bitch have to be pregnant? I wanted to have children with him, but that wasn't in the cards for us. The one time in my life that I became pregnant was at thirteen; my uncle was the father. My aunt took me to have a back-alley abortion so that no one could ever find out, and the doctor botched me up so bad that it was impossible for me to ever have children.

"Stephanie, did you hear what I said?" J.B. asked as he stroked my hair. "Baby, talk to me," he pleaded.

I couldn't form words to speak. It was as if my whole world had just crumbled. Out of all the girls he could've cheated on me with, it had to be Sharie. She could've had any other man in the neighborhood. Shit, everybody wanted her. She was tall and nicely built with skin the color of rich sand. Her medium-length, brown hair hung past her shoulders, and her chestnut-colored eyes were big and bright. She was one of the most beautiful girls in the neighborhood. Why did she have to go after my man? Why did she have to get her hooks into J.B.?

"You promised, J.B. You promised that you would stop seeing her," I sobbed.

"And I did, but the night I ended it, we had sex, and now she's pregnant," he replied.

"How could you do this to me? How?" I queried in a brittle voice.

"I'm sorry for this, Stephanie. All of it." His voice was thick with emotions as he spoke in an apologetic tone. "I have to leave you, Stephanie. I have to be with the mother of my child."

Shaking my head no, I sat up on his lap with tears streaming down my face and a look of desperation.

"No, J. B., you can't leave me. I need you," I sobbed.

"Sharie needs me, and my unborn child needs me even more."

"I need you, J.B. I can help you with your child; I will accept him or her and love them as if they were my own. Whatever I have to do, I'll do it. Just don't leave me, J. B., please," I begged as tears flooded my eyes.

J.B got up from his seat. "I'm sorry, Steph, but I can't do that. I have to go," he said as he grabbed his jacket off the back of his chair.

"No, I won't let you leave. You can't do this to me, J.B., I love you." I was pulling on his shirt, trying to stop him from leaving, but he was too strong for me to hold on too, and I ended up falling on the ground.

I didn't understand why he had to leave me to be with Sharie. They weren't even in a relationship, and he didn't love her like he loved me.

"You think I want to do this, huh? No. I love you too, but I love my unborn child more. I have to do this for that reason alone," he said as he picked me up from the ground and held me tightly.

He let me go then caressed my cheek, staring at me with a look of love mixed with pain. With no words spoken, his gaze told me that he loved me, one last time, before he continued to walk towards the door.

Determined not to let him leave, I jumped in front of the door, still begging him to stay. He quickly pushed me out of the way then stormed out of the doorway, leaving me standing there broken hearted and crying my eyes out.

"Sunny? Sunny, are you alright?" Lanae's perturbed voice snapped me out of my memory.

I looked up at Psycho with tear-filled eyes.

"What's your name?" I asked, trying to get conformation to what I already knew.

"Psycho," he replied, looking at me with confusion written all over his face.

"No, what's your born name?" I inquired.

He looked over at Lanae, pointing at me with raised brows and a look that said you better get her. I chuckled at the look. It was an all too familiar look. I'd seen that look plenty of times.

"Sunny, what's all this about?" Lanae asked just as confused as he was.

"Please, just tell me your name," I pleaded.

Lanae nodded her head. "It's cool, Psycho. Other than you, she's the only person in Memphis that I know I can trust," she assured.

He looked at her then back to me as if he were trying to figure out if he should trust me or not.

"Trust me. I need to know," I spoke slightly above a whisper, hoping that he would hear the desperation in my voice.

He stared into my eyes as if he were looking for a sign to tell him that it was okay for him to tell me his name. Lanae held his hand tightly, and it was as if that were the sign that he was looking for to assure him that he could tell me the truth.

"Yajir Jordan," he answered.

I exhaled the breath that I was holding as I began to feel light headed. I grabbed the back of the chair for support.

"You J.B.'s boy," I acknowledged as I burst into tears.

Lanae and Psycho both were looking at me with identical looks of shock on their faces.

"You knew my father?" he queried.

"Knew your father? Honey, I loved your father," I replied with a huge grin.

Thinking about J.B. and seeing his son brought back so many feelings that I wasn't prepared for. I walked over to the mini bar and poured myself a drink.

"Would you like a drink?" I offered Psycho, knowing that he was probably feeling confused and full of emotions as well.

He nodded his head yes. I grabbed another glass from the cabinet and poured him a drink.

"I met your daddy when I was eighteen years old. That's around your age now," I told him as I passed him his drink.

I motioned him and Lanae to have a seat then walked around the desk to sit in my chair. I opened my antique box and pulled out a blunt, lit it, then took a huge pull. As I blew the smoke out of my mouth, I leaned back, resting my head against my chair.

"You are J.B.'s spitting image when he was your age."

"Yeah, Bruce always say that I'm him all over again. He say I even have his mannerisms."

"Bruce? How the hell is Bruce? Ha-ha! He was my buddy. He was a barrel of laughs."

"He's good, and he's still a trip." Psycho chuckled.

"We sho' did have some good times—me, your daddy, and Bruce," I recalled, taking another hit of the blunt then offering it to Psycho.

"Your daddy was my knight in shinny armor. He saved me."

My heart was heavy and, at the same time, filled with joy. So many wonderful memories were flashing through my mind, and I was starting to feel overwhelmed.

"How did he save you?" Lanae asked.

I shook my head and let out a sigh. "Oh, Lanae, my mini me. I use to call you that for a reason. All those nights we stayed up, having long conversations, talking about our lives, I told you that we were one of the same, but I don't think you fully understood. I endured everything you did, plus more. When my parents died, I had to move in with my grandma. I was twelve years old. My uncle, Garrett, raped me that night, and any other night that he wanted to. My grandma and my Aunts Glady and Glynda knew, but they thought that since he was on drugs, he didn't know what he was doing. They decided to turn the other cheek. By the time I was eighteen, the rapes were more brutal, and he even brought his friends to join him. I had enough, and I decided that it was time for me to leave."

I looked over at Psycho before continuing.

"That's when I met your daddy. I was sitting on the steps of an abandoned apartment building. It was in the dead of winter, and I was freezing my ass off. But I was determined not to go back to my grandmother's house. I pulled my hood over my head and tucked my arms inside my coat, hoping to find a little bit of warmth. I laid my head on my knees and started rocking back and forth, crying. That's when your daddy approached me and asked if I was alright. I looked up; he was standing there, looking just like you right now, waiting for me to answer."

I poured myself another drink, took a sip, and then continued my story.

"I tried to tell him that I was fine, but J.B. wasn't hearing that. He sat down on the step next to me and said, 'I don't like to be lied to, and it's too damn cold for you to be sitting out here crying. Now I'ma sit right here with you and freeze my ass off right along with you until you tell me the truth.' I called his bluff, and after sitting in silence for another half an hour, shivering from the cold, I decided to tell him the truth. He took me in that night, and he helped me get my life on track. We became good friends. No. He was my best friend. Then, we fell in love." I smiled at the memory. "He left me when he found out about you. He wanted to make sure you had a good life. In fact, everything he did after that was for you. He loved you from the moment Sharie told him she was pregnant. He gave up his life and sacrificed so much to make sure you and your mother was good. I respect him for that. Your father was a good man."

He nodded his head. "From what I hear, he was."

"Lanae, take it from me; if he's anything like his daddy, he's a good one," I stated truthfully.

"According to your story, he's exactly like his daddy. He saved me too," she said with a big smile on her face.

She looked happy, and I was happy for her. I never wanted her to make a life out of this lifestyle like I did. I just wanted her to get enough money so that she could go to school and build a life for herself. Do the things that I was never able to do.

"No, she saved me," Psycho avowed, taking Lanae's hand and kissing her cheek.

The look in his eyes when he looked at her was the same look of love that J.B. had in his eyes when he looked at me.

"No matter what your daddy did, that man took care of me until the day he died." I closed my eyes as tears began to fall, and my mind drifted back to the night I found out that J.B. had been killed.

I was on my way home from my part-time job at McDonald's. I heard a lot of commotion coming from the next street over. I didn't pay it any mind at first because shit was always happening around that area. As I was crossing the street, I saw police cars and an ambulance. I got an instant ache in my heart. It was as if something were wrong. I decided to walk down that street, just to see what was going on. I got a sinking feeling in the pit of my stomach as fear washed over me, and I started to feel anxious. My heart was pounding, and I could feel the tiny hairs on my body rise. I sped up my pace as I continued down the street. The closer I got to the commotion, the more anxious I began to feel.

"No, Stephanie, stay back," Bruce warned as he rushed towards me.

My heart had been telling me that something had happened to J.B., and Bruce grabbing me, trying to hold me back, only confirmed what I already knew in my heart. But for some reason, I had to see for myself.

"Let me go, Bruce!" I cried out, struggling to free myself from his grip.

"I can't do that, Stephanie. You don't need to see that," he expressed as he pulled me away.

"Please, Bruce, let me go. I have to see for myself. I have to know," I pleaded as tears spilled from my eyes.

Bruce nodded his head. "Aight, go 'head," he said, releasing me from his grip.

My heart was heavy, and my legs felt like lead as I rushed through the crowd of onlookers.

"You have to stay back behind the tape," the officer instructed as I stepped over the tape.

I ignored him and barged my way past him.

"Ma'am," he called behind me, jogging to catch up with me.

I froze, and my breathing ceased as I watched the paramedics zip J.B.'s lifeless body in a body bag. My legs began to feel like jelly; then, I collapsed onto the pavement. I took one huge gasp of air before letting out a pain-filled scream. The officer touched my shoulders, trying to pull me off the ground.

"Ma'am, are you alright?" he asked.

"I got her," Bruce told him as he knelt beside me and wrapped me into his arms.

"It's okay, Stephanie. Everything's gonna be ok. Come on."

He lifted me off the ground and led me back towards the tape. I looked over his shoulder at J.B., zipped in the body bag, still not believing that he was gone. As my eyes roamed around the area, I noticed that we were in front of a well-known drug house. Then, I spotted Sharie sitting on the ground, looking spaced out and nodding off. Anger took over my body.

"You bitch!" I shouted, trying to run up on her and knock her ass out. *"You fucking crack-headed whore. You didn't deserve him. You low-down, man-stealing whore!"* I raged.

Sharie was high as hell as she continued to stare in space with her head bobbing up and down. Bruce dragged me further down the street and away from the crowd.

"Yo, Stephanie, calm down," he demanded, shaking me lightly.

"He left me for that bitch, and all she did was bring him misery. Now look at her. She's a fucking crack head, and she looks like hell. How could he stay with her, Bruce? Why didn't he come back to me?" I sobbed.

"Come on, Stephanie. Let me take you home," he offered.

"No, I want to walk. I need to walk," I replied.

Bruce nodded in agreement then gave me a hug. I told him that I would call him later then continued down the street with my arms wrapped around my body and my head hanging down, still trying to process the fact that J.B. was dead. As I walked down the block, I saw a sight that made my heart break even more.

I paused. Wiping the tears from my eyes, I took a deep breath then opened my eyes.

"I saw you the night your father died. You was sitting on the steps in your yard with your chin on your knees, dragging a stick through the dirt with tears slowly rolling down your face. You looked lonely and lost. I couldn't understand why no one was holding you, trying to comfort you. It broke my heart. I wanted to wrap my arms around you and tell you that everything would be okay. But before I could move, you shouted, 'I hate you,' and threw the stick in the street. You hopped up so fast and stormed into the house. All I could say was, "there's J.B." One thing about your daddy, as sweet and kindhearted as he was, he had one hell of temper. Don't piss him off, or you would definitely see a side of him you wouldn't like."

Lanae burst into laughter.

"Don't I know." She shook her head. "That's why his name is Psycho. He can be crazy." She chuckled.

Psycho got up, walked over to me, and took my hands in his as he kneeled in front of me.

"My daddy loved you, Stephanie." He winked his eye.

Him mentioning my name through me for a loop. I never told anyone my real name, not even Lanae. I stared at him suspiciously, wondering how he knew my name.

"I overheard Bruce and my daddy talking about a woman named Stephanie a few times before, and you speak about him the same way that he spoke about this woman. I assume you're her," he replied, answering my question before I could form the words to ask.

I nodded my head, acknowledging that he was correct. He winked his eye then stood up.

"Aight, enough of this trip down memory lane. As much as I love hearing stories about my daddy, this is all too much for me. Too damn emotional." He patted the top of my hand and headed back to his seat beside Lanae. "Tell her why we're here," he urged Lanae.

Lanae scooted to the edge of her seat, , and began to speak. Before she could utter a word, I held my hand up to stop her.

"Before you go any further, can I talk to you for a minute? I have something that I need to say to you."

"I'll step out and let you two talk for a minute," Psycho suggested as he got up from his seat.   He gave Lanae a kiss on top of the head then walked out of the office.

"That boy even got that smooth ass walk like J.B.," I said, shaking my head

"What's up? Stephanie," Lanae said jokingly.

I chuckled slightly. "I haven't heard that name in so long."

"Why didn't you ever tell me your name was Stephanie?" she asked.

"Because Stephanie died the night J.B. died. On my way home from the scene, I ran into Panama, and he changed my life forever."

A lone tear fell from my eye, as memories of that night came to surface.

"Thank you, Lanae," I stated in a low tone as I wiped away the tears and looked up at Lanae.

"Thank me for?" she questioned, sounding baffled.

"For killing Panama," I replied.

She shook her head. "Sunny, I didn't—" she started, but I cut her off.

"Don't try to play coy with me, Lanae. I found out what he did to you that night, and you disappeared. Later that night, he turned up dead.

It didn't take rocket science to put two and two together. You don't know how bad I wanted to do that shit myself. What he did to you—that's the real Panama. He's a tyrant. J.B.'s murder tore me apart, and Panama used my broken heart to manipulate me. I thought I was meeting a man I could fall in love with and could take me out of my misery. He had other plans, and he beat me into submission. After that, I played my part and did as I was told. That's how I was able to survive."

"Why didn't you leave?" she questioned as if she were searching for understanding.

"And do what? I had no education, and I didn't know what else to do. And by the time I figured it out, I was too damn old to try to start a career. I decided to learn the business and stay on Panama's good side. Now look at me. I'm head bitch in charge. There was no one else who could keep this place a float, so I took it on, and now, I don't have to suck another dick or let some random ass nigga fuck me any way he wants to get money. I'm making more money than I could have ever imagined. I'm set for life. So again, I thank you."

With no words spoken, Lanae slid closer to me and gave me a hug. After embracing each other for a few more minutes, I let Psycho back in so they could tell me what was going on. I couldn't believe that my little fire cracker, Lanae, was that damn ruthless, and I loved her even more.

"Okay, I will help you. That nigga need to know that he don't fuck with my people and live to tell the tale. I have the perfect girl to put on him. Her name is Kesha, and I can guarantee that if he sees her, he'll flock to her like bees to honey. She has a couple of days off, so in the meantime, let me get you two set up in a place so you can get settled."

"You'll do that for us?" Psycho asked.

I looked at him like he was out of his mind

"On the strength of my love for yo' father and my love for her, I'll do anything for the two of you."

"Thank you, Sunny," he said as I grabbed my keys and a set to one of the houses that Panama kept secret.

"Y'all ready?" I asked.

"Yeah, we ready, but it's one thing I have to ask," Lanae informed as she stood up.

"What?" I asked in a high-pitched voice and raised brows.

"Don't call me Lanae. My name is Ryda now," she stated as she opened the door.

"Okay, Ryda." I chuckled. "It's whatever you want. Shit, I'm riding with you," I said as we headed out of the door.

PSYCHO

"Was that crazy or what?" Ryda asked as we pulled out of the driveway of The House of Angels.

We were following Sunny to the place that she said she had for us to stay. I looked at Ryda with confusion written all over my face. I had no idea what she was referring to. As if she were reading my mind, Ryda chuckled then answered the question in my head before I could even ask it.

"I'm talking about Sunny knowing your dad. Was that shit crazy? I tell you, it's a small fucking world," she replied, shaking her head.

"Yeah, it is a small world, and that shit was crazy as hell. I thought you were on some bullshit when you said you had a plan, but damn, this plan seemed to have landed us with the right damn person. I guess you can call it a win because I had no idea I was gon' find out some more shit about my daddy."

"How do you feel about that? Finding out your father was in love with another woman other that you moms."

"I don't really feel shit. I mean, I really don't know what the hell type of relationship him and that bitch of a mother of mine had. I don't know if it was the drugs or what. All I remember is she was always a bitch towards him, and he was always loving towards her. Shit, like I told you before, I used to catch her cheating, so I really don't know what I feel about that. At the same time, it's a little disappointing knowing that my mother was a side piece, and my daddy was a cheater. I mean, even if she is a bitch."

"Well, Psycho, your dad was human, and he made a mistake. It ain't no reason to hold that against him."

"So if I cheat on you, would that be a mistake?" I asked, hypothetically speaking.

Ryda looked at me with raised brows "Are you trying to tell me something?" she asked in a high-pitch voice.

I couldn't help but laugh at her facial expression.

"No, I was just hypothetically speaking," I replied, shaking my head.

"Well, since we're hypothetically speaking, let me turn that question around on you. Would you see it as a mistake if I was to cheat on you?"

"Hell yeah, it would be a serious mistake on your part. A mistake that might cost you your life," I answered truthfully.

"Ok, well to answer your question. It wouldn't be a wise decision for you to cheat on me. I'll … what's that bitch name?" she snapped her fingers a couple of times to think before continuing. "Oh yeah, Lorena Bobbitt. I'll Lorena Bobbitt your ass."

"Come on, Ryda. Don't joke about my dick. I don't play them types of games," I said as I grabbed my dick, thinking about what Lorena Bobbitt did.

"Who said I was joking?" she asked with her eyebrows raised and lips poked out.

"Aight, drop this convo. You play too damn much," I said as we made a left, onto Belle Meade Lane.

Ryda was laughing so hard she had to hold her stomach. I'm talking about she was slapping her knee and all. I didn't think the shit was that fucking funny. We made a left, onto Poplar Avenue, and I started looking around at the big ass houses, trying to figure out where the hell Sunny was going. She turned on her left signal light then proceeded to turn onto West Cherry Circle.

"Yo, where the hell Sunny ass taking us? Ain't shit over here but some rich muthafuckas that I would love to stick up."

"I don't know. Maybe she's making a stop first," Ryda replied, looking out the window at all the beautiful houses.

Sunny pulled up to a closed gate that sat in front of a big ass house with a circle driveway. She got out of the car and punched in a code. The gate opened, and then Sunny got back into her car and headed up the driveway. We followed her to the front of the house. She shut her engine off then got out of the car. I decided not to turn my engine off because I had no intensions of following her into whoever's house that was.

"Y'all coming or what?" she questioned, standing in front of my car with her hands on her hips.

Ryda rolled down her window and told her to go ahead and take care of her business, and we would wait in the car. Sunny started laughing hard. Ryda and I were confused. Neither one of us understood what the hell she was laughing at.

"Get y'all asses out of the car. This is where y'all staying." She chuckled, pointing at the big ass house.

Ryda and I both stared at each other with wide eyes, surprised that this was the house she had for us to stay in.

"Shit, I feel like the Jefferson's right now 'cause we definitely just moved on up to the east side." Ryda chuckled.

"Get yo' ass out the car, with yo' crazy ass." I laughed, shutting the engine off then opening the car door.

She laughed then got out the car, singing the theme song to the TV show. I shook my head then stepped out of the car.

"Girl, what the hell you dancing and singing The Jefferson's for?" Sunny asked as she threw her arm around Ryda's neck.

"Sunny, pay her silly ass no attention. She ain't wrapped to tight," I answered.

"Nope, I can't be sane fucking around with your crazy ass," Ryda replied as she playfully punched my arm

Sunny shook her head, laughing, as we headed into the house. Walking into that house felt like I'd stepped into another world. I'd never seen anything so damn beautiful in my life. It was spacious, bright, and airy. It had tall ceilings and hardwood floors throughout. The living room was vaulted and had beams on the ceiling. The kitchen was open and had all new appliances.

"Damn, Sunny, this shit is nice as hell," I expressed, looking out of the wall of windows at the backyard.

Those windows brought in so much natural light that it lit up the whole house. We walked out to the backyard, and I almost fell the fuck out. Not only was the backyard huge, but it had an in-ground swimming pool with a large waterfall fountain spilling over into the pool. I looked over to the right and noticed the outdoor kitchen, complete with a big ass grill and a smoker.

"Hell muthafuckin' yeah!" I shouted as I rushed over to the area to admire the grill. I felt like a kid in a candy store. I couldn't wait to throw some fat ass steaks on that grill.

"Aye, babe, this the type of shit we deserve. I'ma make that shit happen for us one day," I said with a raised voice and outstretched arms, letting her know that I was talking about the house.

Sunny walked over to the outside bar and poured us some drinks. Ryda grabbed my hand and led me over to the bar to join Sunny.

"I'm glad y'all like the place. It's already paid for, so feel free to stay here as long as you want. I've kept up with the bill payments, and I will continue to do so, so don't worry about if you can afford the bills. If you decide that you want to stay here once y'all get on your feet, we can work out some type of arrangement," Sunny told us.

"For real?" I questioned

"Look, I don't really use this house anymore. I was thinking about selling it or renting it out anyway, so it's yours for as long as you want it." She shrugged her shoulders then handed me the keys.

"Thank you, Sunny, for everything," Ryda said, reaching over the bar to give Sunny a hug.

"Girl, no need to thank me. You know I got y'all back." Sunny kissed Ryda then me on the forehead. "Ok, I'ma get out of here and let y'all get settled. Y'all might have to go to the store for groceries. Do y'all need any money?"

"Naw, we good on that," I replied.

"Alright then. I'll see y'all tomorrow." She waved at us as she walked across the yard and into the house.

I grabbed Ryda by the waist and pulled her in for an embrace. She wrapped her arms around my neck then planted a kiss on my lips.

"Baby, I'm dead ass. You deserve to live in something like this. I don't know about staying in here, in Memphis, but I promise you'll have a house like this or nicer one day," I promised.

"Psycho, as long as I'm with you, it don't matter where we live. Shit, I'll live in a cardboard box with you," she replied before kissing me passionately.

"I don't know about that. I ain't about to live in no damn cardboard box." I chuckled.

Ryda mushed my head then said, "Shut up and let's go to the store. I know your ass hungry."

"Hell yeah. That damn grill got a nigga's mouth watering for a big juicy ass steak," I admitted.

Ryda shook her head. "I got your juicy ass steak." She giggled, walking towards the house.

I jogged to catch up with her. Grabbing her ass with both hands, I gave her cheeks a nice squeeze.

"Oh, I'ma get some of that juicy shit later tonight. Shit, this a big ass house, and it got a lot of rooms that we need to try out."

Ryda punched me in my chest then ran into the house. I chased her into the house and to the kitchen. I caught up to her and grabbed her around her waist.

"Shit, we can start right here, in the kitchen, right now."

Lifting her up by her waist, I placed her on the top of the island.

"Psycho, we have to go to the store now. You said you hungry, right?" she   questioned, trying to push me away.

"Fuck that. The only thing I need to eat right now is you," I replied as I planted moist kisses on her neck.

"No, what you need to do now is stop fucking around, and let's go to the store," she responded, trying to push me off her again.

I pushed her back against the counter then pulled her to the edge. I started tugging at the button on her jeans.

"Quit it, Psycho. We need to go to the store," she said, trying to free her legs.

I ignored her and continued taking down her jeans and panties. She continued protesting, and I continued to ignore her as I unbuttoned my jeans, letting them fall to my ankles. I placed her legs on my shoulders then plunged deep inside of her, making her scream my name.

"Damn, I need that steak asap," I said as I grabbed a handful of paper towel and wetted them so we could wash up a little.

Ryda was still laid out on the island top, trying to recover from the quickie we just had. I was pounding that ass, ninety going north, making her ass scream and nut all over the place.

"Girl, get yo' loud ass off that counter and let's get to this store so I can come back and take a shower. Screaming all loud like somebody was murdering yo' ass." I snickered, grabbing her hand to help her off the counter.

"Shit, it felt like you was trying to," she said, putting on her clothes

"Only thing I was murdering was that fat ass, juicy ass pussy of yours." I winked at her. "That was just a teaser; the real shit gon' come later. Now, get the molasses out yo' ass, and let's go," I continued, slapping her ass as I mimicked Ike Turner in the movie *What's Love Got to Do with It*.

She slid on her jeans and her shoes, and then we headed to the grocery store. Even though I was feeling relaxed, Cutty's ass was still weighing heavy on my mind. I couldn't believe our relationship had gotten   to   this   point.

CUTTY

"So that's the type of bullshit you on now, nigga?" I asked Trip as I entered the room of the trap house.

My crew was chilling and acting as if they didn't have a care in the world. Word on the street was that one of my workers had been running their mouth about hitting up Yajir's spot, and now, I had to straighten shit out.

"What you talking about, Cutty? What bullshit?" he questioned, looking confused.

Shaking my head while pinching my nose, trying to contain my anger, I let out a slight chuckle.

"Running yo' got damn mouth; that's what the fuck I'm talking about. You running 'round here, bragging about hitting Yajir's spot?" I looked at him with disgust before snatching that nigga up by his collar.

"What the fuck wrong with you?" I yelled, slamming him against the wall. "Don't you know lose lips sink ships, muthafucka?" I was mad as hell. I was so close to this nigga's face yelling. I swear, spit was flying out of my mouth and on his face.

"Dumbass muthafucka!" I shouted as I mushed his head against the wall.

"Yo, Cutty, calm down," Kayo said, trying to pull me off the nigga.

"Man, get the fuck off me!" I snarled, snatching away from him, then stomping over to the table, and grabbing the bottle of Hennessey.

"That nigga, Yajir, roams the fuckin' streets all fuckin' day and night. You think that shit not gonna get to him? You think that nigga gon' just lay down and let us fuck him? Fuck no! Y'all seen the tape. Ain't none of us think that nigga was as ruthless as he is."

I gulped down the drink that I poured, trying to calm myself down.

"So what? Yajir got you shook, Cutty?" Trip snickered, standing against the wall, looking all disheveled and shit, mugging me like he was about to pop off.

The lil' smirk he was displaying along with that dumbass comment he made, only infuriated me even more. With balled fists, I stormed towards him.

"Nigga, you gon' do something? You feeling froggy, muthafucka?" I questioned, looking him up and down, returning the same mean mug he had on his face.

"Man, Cutty, it ain't got to be all this. I was just telling a few homeboys of mine what went down. That's all."

"That's all? That's all! Nigga, running yo' muthafuckin' mouth can get us all hemmed up. Fuck you mean *that's all*? I oughta knock yo' bitch ass out." I bucked at the nigga with my fist balled.

"One thing I'm not is a bitch, so I suggest you kill that shit. I only let that shit you did a few minutes ago slide 'cause I understand you mad, and I may have made a mistake, but you ain't getting no more passes."

I couldn't believe this lil' muthafucka called himself bossing up on me, talking 'bout I ain't getting no more passes. I laughed in the nigga's face right before I punched in it, splitting his shit. His mouth was leaking as his body hit the floor.

"Don't … you … ever … in your life … try to … step … to me." I kicked him with every word.

"Enough, Cutty. He had enough."

Kayo pulled me away from Trip, knowing that if he didn't stop me, I would've stomped a mud hole in that lil' nigga.

"Clean yo' bitch ass up and get the fuck out my shit," I spat as I straightened out my clothes.

"Next one of y'all muthafuckas wanna run yo' mouth, remember my example, and rethink yo' decision," I warned them before storming out the door.

"Look, man, I ain't wanna say nothing, but what about yo' girl? I mean, how well do you really know her? Where you meet her at?"

"Naw, man, my girl ain't do that shit."

"I'm just saying; bitches be doing some sheisty ass shit. I wouldn't put nothing past her. All I'm saying is think about it. I mean, who else knows where you live?"

"I ain't gotta think about shit. My girl rides for me."

"Shit, are you sure, my nigga? It seems to me that she rides for herself. Her telling those niggas she was pregnant only made them fuck with yo' mind and use her against you. The way I see it—she was only out for self."

"Naw, she can't be that stupid."

"What, nigga?"

"Nothing. Look, man, let me get outta here. I got some shit to do."

The last conversation I had with that nigga, Yajir, played through my mind as I drove down the street, heading to my house. I slipped up and said something pertaining to Ryda that I shouldn't have said. Yajir never gave me full details of what happened that night my boys hit his crib. My boys did. That was how I knew Ryda tried that lame ass 'I'm pregnant' shit, and if I could figure out that I'd had a slip of the tongue, so could he. I was glad the niggas head was so fucked that night that he didn't realize that I slipped up right then and there, 'cause I would've had to kill him off the top, and I would hate to have had to do that shit in my own home.

I pulled up to my house and started looking around for any signs of Yajir. I had to make sure his ass wasn't hiding in the cut somewhere. See, I knew how he moved. When we were younger, we were stick-up boys together, and Yajir was the mastermind. He planned each hit out carefully and was very calculated in his planning. We would watch all the niggas on the block getting paper for at least a week to see who was making the most money. That was the one Yajir decided that we would stick up. We would stay in the cut, watching the nigga make his money, and at the end of the night, we would come out of the cut and rob the nigga. That was all Yajir's plan, so when I saw his mother on the news and heard the detail of the crime, there was no doubt in my mind that he did that shit, and I wanted in.

Grabbing my gun from under the seat, I made sure it was loaded and ready just in case Yajir thought that he could lay in the cut and catch me slipping. I didn't want to go to war with the nigga for real. All I was trying to do was make him have no choice but to make his next move, and I planned on being there to see how he operated. I tried to get him to confess to the robberies the night we talked about his mother's appearance on the news, but the nigga sat in my face and lied. Just like him, I hate to be lied to. My daddy used to lie to me constantly. *I'ma come and get you this weekend. I'ma get you them shoes you want. I'll call you later.* Those were just a few of the many lies he told me.

I thought Yajir and I were at least on the same page about getting money, so I figured that if he were hitting these spots, we could do that shit as a team and maybe upgrade to bigger and better spots. But this muthafucka lied to me. I had no choice but to do the shit my way. But watching him on that tape of the liquor store, I saw something different in him. I saw something that I'd never seen before. Yajir was a ruthless killer, and I knew now that I couldn't sleep on him.

"This nigga has got to really be insane," I mumbled to myself as I looked around, heading into my house, thinking about the way his eyes looked when he killed the liquor store owners.

He looked as if he were getting satisfaction out of the shit, and the way he had Ryda playing like she was just another customer and flirting with them niggas was genius. At first, I didn't realize it was her, being that I'd never met her, but I was smart, and it didn't take long for me to figure that shit out. At first glance, it looked like she left the store as soon as he approached the counter, but I noticed the look on the nigga's face in the back. When he glanced to the right, he looked scared to death. I rewound the tape over, and over, again. The only thing I could figure out was Ryda must've been on the side of the of the counter with a gun pointed at him.

"Them niggas should've had their camera positioned better," I tittered as I sat on my couch to roll a blunt.

About halfway through facing my jay and drinking two glasses of Henny, somebody started banging on my door. I looked at the time and noticed that it was half passed midnight. The only person who knew my schedule and popped up at my house was Yajir. I grabbed my gun off the table and held it at my side just in case this nigga was on some funny shit.

"Who the fuck is it?" I shouted as I approached the door with my finger on my trigger.

"It's me, Cutty! Kayo," Kayo replied.

The frantic sound of his voice let me know that something had gone down, and I wasn't sure if I really wanted to know what. I let out a frustrated sigh, placed my gun in the small of my back, and then swung my door open.

"Yo, Cutty, man, this shit is wild. I can't believe this shit," Kayo excitedly spoke as he stormed through my door.

He was breathing heavily, pacing my floor with his hands on top of his head and a look of panic on his face.

"It all happened so fast. I mean, these niggas came out of nowhere.

It was like some shit you see in the movies. I barely escaped with my own life. I didn't see these muthafuckas coming. It's like they were following us or knew our routine or something," he rambled, and I had no clue what he was talking about.

"Aye, calm down, nigga, and tell me what the fucks going on," I contributed as I passed that nigga the blunt.

He took a couple of hits from the blunt then sat down.

"Man, Trip and Mo is dead," he told me.

I was in shock. I just left them niggas moments ago and now they dead. I couldn't believe my ears.

"What the fuck you just say, nigga?" I questioned for clarity.

"You heard me; Trip and Mo is dead," he repeated.

"What the fuck!" I exclaimed. "Tell me what the hell happened?"

"Man, I don't fucking know. We left the trap and went to the burger joint down the block. We parked in our usual spot in the back. As soon as we got out of the car and started to walk towards the back of the building, like three niggas in a black truck pulled up and started banging on us. We didn't even have time to pull out our straps. Mo and Trip was a little ahead of me and Cliff; they got hit. Me and Cliff both ducked and pulled out our shit. But by the time the shooting stopped, those niggas were ghost."

"Did you see who these niggas was?" I asked still surprised.

"I saw them, but I don't know who the fuck these niggas was. I never saw them muthafuckas before. They was in and out fast as shit," he replied.

I sat in silence, thinking of who in the hell tried to roll on my crew. I rolled another blunt then put that shit in the air. I needed to calm myself down so that I could think straight.

"Cutty, what the fuck we gon' do?" Kayo asked.

Still trying to wrap my head around what he had just told me, I couldn't respond.

"Cutty," he called.

As I continued to think, I came to only one conclusion. Yajir was behind this shit, and that meant he knew that I was involved in hitting his shit.

"This what we gon' do. I need eyes on Yajir's crib at all times. I need to know when he comes and goes. I need him followed. I need to know where he goes, and who he sees. If he coming after me, I have to get him before he gets me. If it's war he wants, then that's what he gets—no holds barred."

Kayo told me that he would get on it then he left my house. I finished the blunt that I started then took a shower and went to bed with nothing but killing Yajir on my mind.

RYDA

Sitting in the house, watching TV and waiting for Psycho to return, had me thinking about my mother. She would sit in the house all day, cooking, cleaning, and watching TV while the dead man would be out doing who knows what. It was ok for him to leave her in the house like that when he was at work, but he left her in the house all day most of the time. He almost never came straight home after work, and on the weekends, when he didn't work, he would be gone all day and never took her anywhere. I guess that was a good thing because we were always walking on egg shells, wondering what mood he was gonna come home in. Shit, maybe I should say that we were treading on water because if he came home with the slightest attitude, we were all gonna drown.

The fucked up part about all of this was the dead man wasn't a drunk or anything. He was sober most of the time that he'd terrorized us. At least if he had a substance abuse problem, he would've had a reason for being so damn surly, even though it wouldn't have excused his behavior. And I truly do not understand what it was that made him so angry. He had a good job, a nice house, great kids, and a beautiful, loving wife. Still, it seemed as if nothing was ever good enough for him.

My mother was a sweet woman, but he beat her down so bad that she no longer had her own personality. She would do whatever he said and act however he wanted her to act. Even that wasn't enough to stop him from beating the shit out of her. When the dead man got in his mood, no one was safe. I guess that was why she looked the other way whenever he came after me or my brothers. Since I was the only person in the house that tried to stand up to him, I got it the worst. The bruises I sustained from his physical abuse, in time, healed, but the scar that was left on my heart was permanent, and time would never heal that.

Unlike most men that molested children, the dead man didn't have to sneak in my room late at night to rape me. He did it whenever he felt like it, and my mother would act as if she didn't see or hear anything no matter how loud I screamed and cried. And when he was finished, he would go right back downstairs to a hot meal like nothing had happened. She didn't have the decency to come upstairs and check on me. Not one time did my mother ever try to stop the dead man. If she had, maybe I would have had mercy on her. Maybe I would have let her live.

I grabbed my phone off the coffee table, unlocked it, and then logged into my fake Instagram and scrolled to my brother Raymond's page. I clicked on the video that he posted of my little brother, Davion, that he made on one of their weekly visits with him. Davion started laughing, and my heart melted. I always loved his cute, little laugh. As I wiped away the tears that were now falling, I had to laugh. Davion was making a silly monkey face and trying to imitate the sound that monkey's make.

"You silly little monkey." I giggled as I slowly traced his face on the screen.

Suddenly, I heard one of the most horrific sounds that I'd ever heard. My brother Raymond chuckled as he began speaking, sounding as if he were extremely happy. I cringed at the sound. As much as I loved my brother Davion, I hated my brother Raymond. He was the perfect spawn of the dead man. I quickly hit pause on the video then swiped it away. The last thing I needed to hear or see was that evil muthafucka being happy.

"I hate you, Raymond, and I can't wait to show you how much," I murmured, tossing the phone back on the table as I sat back on the couch and took a deep breath.

The warm feeling that I had in my heart turned cold. It wasn't like I was heartless; it was just that the things that were allowed to happen to me in that house made it almost impossible for me to feel anything at all. The only time I felt anything was when I was with Psycho. He'd added so much to my life; I couldn't imagine living without him. Just thinking about him brought joy to my heart, and a mile-wide smile to my face. When he wasn't around me, I missed him so damn much. I snatched the phone off the table again then called him. I sat back with one arm folded across my mid-section and my legs crossed, waiting for Psycho to answer the phone. It rang three times, and I was starting to get pissed.

"I know you better answer this—" I was cut off by Psycho's voice answering the phone.

"Yeah, go 'head. Finish what you was saying. I better do what?" He chuckled.

"Ummm. ... What you doing?" I asked, trying to skip the subject.

"Umm hmm, keep talking shit. Anyway, I'm finishing up now. Why? You miss me?" he questioned, sounding sexy as hell.

"I was just wondering if you was finished. You been gone for hours," I replied, playing with a string on the couch pillow.

"Ryda, I been gone two hours. Stop acting like I been gone all damn day. You just ready for me to come home and dick you down; that's all that is. You want me to finish what I started in the kitchen earlier," he replied.

"Please. That's what you want. I just wanted to know what you was doing." I laughed.

"Whatever. I'll be home shortly. Love you."

"Love you." I ended the call then went in the kitchen to make myself some tea.

Another hour and a half had come and gone, and Psycho still wasn't home. I was starting to get worried. I picked up the phone and tried to call him again, but it went straight to voicemail. My heart started pounding in my chest, and an eerie feeling rushed over me and landed in the pit of my stomach.

"Come on, Psycho. What are you doing?" I whispered as I tried to call him again.

The phone went straight to voicemail again. I laid back on the couch and started flipping through the channels, looking to see if there were any breaking news stories or anything. This shit with Cutty had my mind all over the place, and it was starting to drive me crazy. I'd never worried about Psycho this much, and I knew it was because I didn't know what

Cutty may be doing.

What if he knew that Psycho figured out that he was behind the robbery? What if he was after Psycho?

Trying to shake those thoughts out of my head, I picked up the phone and called Psycho again. All I needed was to hear his voice and know that he was ok. Again, the phone went straight to voicemail. Trying to rid myself of the worried feelings, I decided to call Sunny. I bit my nails and bounced my knee while I waited for her to answer the ringing phone.

"Hey, Lanae! Oops, I mean, Ryda." She giggled, answering the phone.

"Hey, Sunny," I tittered.

"What's up? You and Psycho enjoying the house?" she questioned.

"Well, he not here so…" I replied as I folded my knees under myself to get comfortable.

"Where he at?" she asked.

I shook my head and took a deep breath before answering.   "He went to the house to get some of our things, but that was hours ago, and he ain't come back yet," I answered.

"You sound worried," she said.

"I am," I admitted.

"I'm sure it ain't nothing to worry about. Psycho won't do anything to put himself in harm's way, I'm sure."

"You don't know him, Sunny. He ain't wrapped to tight, and he would put himself in harm's way if needed. I been calling him, and his phone going straight to voicemail. For real, what if something happened to him? I'll die if it did."

"Girl, calm your over-dramatic ass down. I'm sure Psycho is fine. Why the hell you got to go straight to something happened to him? His phone could be dead or anything else. Chill the hell out. Take a drink or something. I'm sure he'll be walking through the door soon."

"He better, or I'm gon' kill him," I responded.

I knew Sunny was only trying to reassure me, but honestly, that phone call was doing nothing but irritating the hell out of me.

"Well, I'ma get off this phone. I'll talk to you later. Bye," I snapped.

"Ok, lil' Miss Attitude, I'll talk to you later. Go try to relax."

We ended the call. I went upstairs to get a blanket out of the closet so that I could curl up on the couch and wait for Psycho.

PSYCHO

As I was putting the last bag of clothes in the car, my phone started to ring. Already knowing it was Ryda, I decided to wait until I got situated in the car to return her call. I placed the bag in the seat then pulled my phone out of my pocket and checked the missed call. I was shocked to see that it was Bruce calling, not Ryda. Bruce didn't usually call unless he needed me to come by the shop, and it was after midnight, so I had no idea what the hell he wanted. I closed the back door then headed around to the driver's side to get in and call him back. I put my seatbelt on as I waited for him to answer my call.

"Where you at, Yajir?" he answered without greeting me.

"I'm at my apartment. Why? What's up?" I asked baffled by the serious tone in his voice.

"Look, listen to what I'm about to say. Get Ryda, and get the hell out of there. I need you to come here or go somewhere and lay low for a while," he demanded with a hint of urgency in his voice.

I wasn't dumb, and I knew that niggas on the street talked in circles when something serious was going down. But I didn't know what the fuck was going on. All I knew was Bruce sounded alarmed. And to me, that meant that Ryda and I were in danger.

"What's going on, Bruce?" I inquired.

"Not now, Yajir. I need you to do what I said and hit me tomorrow. We need to talk," he stated.

"Aight, me and Ryda good. We got a spot. I'll shoot you the address tomorrow, and you can come talk to me there."

"Aight, lay low, you hear me?" he said.

"I got it," I replied before ending the call.

My mind was racing, trying to figure out what the hell was going on. I knew whatever it was had something to do with Cutty, and it was starting to drive me crazy.

"Yo, what the fuck!" I shouted as I banged my fist on the steering wheel. I leaned my head against the seat and took a few breaths. "What the fuck did I do to this nigga to make him start fucking with me?" I mumbled to myself.

I ain't never did shit to this nigga. Shit, other than the bodies I put down for my own survival, I ain't never do shit to no muthafuckin' body.

Why in the hell do Cutty want beef with me? I thought, but no matter how many times I searched my brain for answers, I couldn't seem to find one.

"Man, fuck!" I shouted as I headed out of the apartment complex.

A million and one thoughts were running through my mind. I had to do something to rid myself of those thoughts so that I could have a clear mind. I decided that instead of going straight to the house, I would put on my music and go for a long drive. I hooked my phone up to the car stereo system then put on my old-school playlist. I reached in my pocket and pulled out the half of jay that I smoked earlier, lit it up, and took a few puffs. As I smoked my jay and bobbed my head to the music, the song was interrupted by the ringing of my phone. I looked at the ID; it was Ryda. I didn't feel like dealing with her at the time, so I rejected her call. She called right back. I didn't know why I didn't think that she would. This time, when I rejected her call, I turned the phone off.

"Fuck it. I'll listen to the radio," I mumbled to myself as I tossed the phone on the passenger seat.

As I continued my drive, I started thinking about my situation. I didn't have no money, and I had Ryda and Sunny both trying to take care of me. That shit couldn't happen. I was a man, and no man should ever allow a woman to take care of him.

"Fuck that shit. I got to get some money now," I said in low voice.

I continued to drive a few more miles then pulled into a gas station. I parked in the darkest parking space then waited for the few cars at the pump to disappear. I watched the people in store gather their items and head to the counter. It was only one worker on the inside. Once the store was clear and the gas pumps were all empty, I grabbed my gun out of the console then pulled my hood over my head. With my gun at my side, I made my way to the door.

"Put yo' got damn hands up, nigga!" I shouted as I entered the store with my gun drawn.

He threw his hands in the air and backed away from the register.

"Who else in the store?" I inquired.

"No one. It's just me," he nervously replied.

I walked behind the counter and grabbed the nigga by the back of his neck. "Nigga, get your ass over here." I pulled him closer to me and pressed the gun to the back of his head.

"Move," I ordered, pushing him towards the back.

I glanced out of the door to make sure no one was coming before going into the back. I checked all the rooms and the bathroom to make sure that the attendant wasn't lying to me. Then, I took him back to the register.

"Open the got damn register," I instructed.

"I can't unless I ring something up," he replied, sounding as if he were about to cry.

I looked at the nigga like he'd lost his got damn mind then grabbed a pack of White Owls off the shelf.

"Ring this shit up, bitch," I commanded.

The attendant did as he was told. Once the register was open, I made him move to the side, and I took all the money.

"Where the fuck is your security tape?" I asked, pointing the gun at the tip of his nose.

"We don't have one. I swear," he answered.

He was breathing hard and sweating bullets. I grabbed him by the throat, pressing the gun under his eye.

"You bet not be lying to me; I hate liars," I said through tight jaws.

"I swear, I'm not lying. It broke years ago. The owner keeps the equipment so it can look like we have cameras. Please believe me. I'm telling the truth," he explained.

The frightened look in his eyes along with the distress in his voice made me believe that he was telling the truth. However, I didn't trust shit. I yanked the nigga by his collar then took him to the back office to search for the tape. He wasn't lying. I found recording devices, but none of them were on. I searched them anyway and found no tape. I looked at the scared attendant then hit him on the head with the butt of my gun. He fell on the floor, and I stood over him and pistol whipped him until he was unconscious, and then, I sent a bullet right between his eyes.

As I was leaving the office, I heard the door chime.

Fuck! I thought before I eased my way out of the door, locking it behind me. With my gun raised, I planted my back flat against the wall and continued easing my way to the back door. I peeked through the opening to make sure that the customers didn't notice me. They weren't paying attention to shit but what they were looking for. I quietly eased out of the back door. I waited, on the side of the building, until the two cars that were at the pumps pulled away, and then, I quickly hopped in my car and sped out of the parking lot.

Once I was a good distance away from the gas station, I turned on my phone to call Ryda to let her know that I was on my way. But when I saw that I had a few missed calls from her, I decided that I would deal with her when I got to the house. When I got in the house, Ryda was curled up on the couch, wrapped in a blanket, sleeping. I quietly crept up the steps so that I could take a quick shower.

After putting the money that I got from the gas station away, I reached in the duffle bag that I brought in with me and pulled out a t-shirt, basketball shorts, boxers, and socks then headed in the bathroom to take a shower. That damn shower was huge and had shower heads coming from the top, the front, and the sides. I turned all of them bitches on and stepped inside. What was supposed to be a quick fifteen to twenty-minute shower turned into an hour-long shower. That damn shower was refreshing as hell, but it had me feeling so relaxed that all I wanted to do was curl up next to my baby and fall right to sleep.

After showering and dressing, I headed downstairs to curl up next to Ryda. She was sleeping so peacefully, and I really didn't want to disturb her. Being as careful as I could, I slid on the couch beside her. She let out a low moan as she shuffled to readjust herself. She slowly blinked her eyes open.

"It's me, baby. I'm home," I said as I kissed her on the side of her head.

"Where you been?" she asked in a groggy voice.

"Shhh, just go back to sleep. We can talk in the morning," I told her, laying my head on the pillow with hers.

"No, Psycho. I was worried. Where you go?" she questioned.

"Go to sleep. We can talk in the morning. Now close your eyes before I fuck you to sleep," I warned her.

She looked at me with furrowed brows as her eyes darted from side to side as if she were searching my eyes for answers. Without saying a word, she slowly closed her eyes.

"Too late," I whispered as I started kissing on her ear then her neck.

I stroked the side of her cheek, brushing her hair behind her ear. I kissed her passionately as I maneuvered my body on top of hers.

****

The next morning, I was awakened by the smell of sausages being cooked. I sat on the side of the couch and rolled me a blunt.

"Time for a little wake and bake," I said to myself as I lit the blunt. I took a few puffs, then headed to the kitchen to see what the hell Ryda was in there whipping up.

"Damn, baby, you got a nigga's stomach growling like shit. What the hell you in here cooking," I asked as I entered the kitchen with the blunt dangling from my mouth. I wrapped my arms around her waist from behind as I peeked over her shoulder to see what she was cooking.

"I'm making biscuits with sausage and gravy, grits, and homemade hash browns," she replied.

"Shit, yo' ass don't be faking in the kitchen, do you?" I chuckled before kissing her on the neck then slapping her ass.

"That dick I gave you last night got yo' ass in a good mood, huh?" I asked, pressing my rod against her ass.

"Boy, go somewhere with that shit. I cook for your ass anyway." She giggled.

"Yeah, right. I bet if I wasn't slanging this dick right, yo' ass wouldn't be in here whipping up this meal," I pointed out.

"Why can't I be in here cooking 'cause I love you? Why your dick got to be the reason?" she questioned.

"'Cause, this a big muthafucka," I stated, grabbing a handful of my tool.

"Get the hell out of my kitchen." She laughed, shaking her head.

I left the kitchen and went back to the living room to spark my blunt back up. As soon as I sat on the couch, Bruce was calling my phone.

"What's up, Bruce?" I answered.

"Nigga, shoot me the address where you at, and I'm on my fucking way," he replied before hanging up on me.

I looked at the phone like the nigga was crazy then texted him the address. About twenty minutes later, Ryda was coming out of the kitchen with my plate, and Bruce was knocking on the door.

"Oh yeah, Bruce coming over," I told her as I headed to the door to open it.

"Well, got damn, nigga. Yo' ass hit the lottery or something. Who the fuck crazy enough to let yo' ass stay in a house like this?" Bruce inquired, walking through the door.

"What's up, man?" I chuckled as I gave him dap.

Bruce looked over my shoulder and noticed Ryda standing there. "Well, hello, gorgeous," he spoke as he pushed me to the side.

"Ryda, this Bruce. Bruce, this Ryda," I introduced.

He took Ryda's hand and kissed it. "It's nice to finally meet you. You are stunning," he said.

"Thank you," she replied, grinning.

"Boy, if I was twenty years younger—" he started.

"You'll still be too old." I laughed, cutting him off as I took Ryda's hand out of his.

"Shit, you should've seen ole Bruce back in my hay days. I couldn't keep the chicks off me. I had to damn near beat them off with sticks to keep them away. I tell you, I was a chick magnet in my younger years. Shit, J.B. was too. We was some hell-raisers, I tell you."

Ryda and I both shook our heads, laughing at Bruce's brief trip down memory lane.

"You want anything to eat or drink? We was just sitting down for breakfast," she offered.

"I'm good on the food, but anything you have to drink with alcohol in it is fine with me," he stated.

Ryda giggled then headed to the kitchen to fix Bruce a drink. I led him to the living room so I could eat, and we could talk about whatever he needed to talk about.

"Yajir, that's a lovely lil' gal you got. You better hold on to her. Ole Bruce might have to snatch her up." He chuckled.

"If you don't sit yo' old ass down." I laughed.

We walked over to the couch and sat down. Bruce's eyes grew two sizes bigger when he saw my plate.

"Got damn, nigga, what you got there? I think I just changed my mind about that plate." He rubbed his stomach and licked his lips. "Aye,

Ryda, I changed my mind! Fix ole Bruce a plate. That sausage gravy look gooder than a muthafucka!" he shouted.

"I got you, old man," she replied, chuckling.

"Aight, nigga. Stop pushing up on my girl and tell me what the hell you here for," I said, sopping up the sausage gravy with a piece of biscuit.

"I'ma get straight to the point. Whatever plan you have for Cutty; you need to put that shit in motion, now. Me and a couple of cats I know hit his crew last night. We got word that he was with them niggas, but when we got to them, his ass was nowhere in sight. I still got eyes on his crew, and I found out this morning that one of them is sitting on your crib. My thoughts are that Cutty got them watching you."

Ryda came back in the living room with Bruce's plate and drink.

"So, that nigga trying to have eyes on us now? He must got some big balls, or he scared as hell. Either way, we got him." She cut in.She passed Bruce his plate, and sat his drink on the table. Then she sat down beside me, and grabbed her plate. I looked at her like she'd lost her mind as sheh put a forkful of food in her mouth. She looked up at me.

"Oh, my bad, I guess this is a man's conversation," she said as she got up off the couch. "I'll be in the kitchen if y'all need me," she added as she kissed me on the cheek.

As we continued the conversation, there was a knock on the door. Bruce grabbed his gun and cocked it.

"I got it!" Ryda shouted, rushing from the kitchen.

I heard her unlocked the locks, and then the sensor chimed, letting me know that she opened the door.

"Good morning," Sunny's cheerful voice came blaring through the hallway.

"I know that voice anywhere," Bruce mentioned as he stood up from his seat.

As soon as Sunny rounded the corner, she stopped in her tracks. Her eyes were wide and full of excitement.

"Is that my nigga, Bruce?" She dropped her big ass purse on the floor and ran into his arms.

"Got dammit, Stephanie. Look at you. You ain't change a bit. You still look good." He beamed as he twirled her around.

"How long has it been now, Bruce? Like fifteen years or so?" she questioned, grinning.

"Shit if I know. All I know is it's been too damn long. Let me look at you again, girl." He took her hand as started spinning her around again. "Mmm, mmm, mmm," he added, giving her the once over.

"Bruce, stop being fresh. You still an old dog." She giggled. "Did he tell y'all he was a low-down dog back in the day?" she asked.

"Not low down enough. I couldn't get you." Bruce winked and flashed her half smile.

"Please. J.B. would've killed both of us." She giggled.

Bruce shook his head, laughing. "Shit, ain't that the truth? J.B. was one crazy ass muthafucka, and he didn't play about his woman. That was my brother, though. I miss the shit out of him still." Bruce shook his head.

"Sounds like somebody I know," Ryda mentioned, rolling her eyes at me.

"Aight, enough of this reminiscing shit. We got shit to handle," I said, breaking up the little flirting secession between Bruce and Sunny.

"We can discuss business in a minute. Right now, I want to know how in the hell did y'all get hooked up with this hell cat?" Bruce inquired.

"Forget that, Bruce. Like Psycho said, we got business to discuss," Sunny said as she led Ryda and me over to the couch.

SUNNY

"Psycho? Nigga, yo' name is Yajir. Where the fuck you get Psycho from?" Bruce asked with a confused look on his face.

Psycho shrugged his shoulders as he sat on the couch.   "It's my name. That bitch of a mother—" he started, but Bruce threw his hands up and stopped him.

"Now, hold on, Yajir. I don't tolerate no disrespecting yo' moms. Kill that shit right now, son," Bruce spoke to Psycho with authority like he was scolding him.

"Naw, Bruce, no disrespect to you, but she don't deserve respect from me. She said I was psycho, just like my dead ass daddy, so that's who I'll be. And I wear the name proudly," Psycho stated.

"Look, son. Now I know yo' momma on that shit, and I know she ain't been the perfect mother, but she did the best she could. She still yo' momma; she deserves respect," Bruce told him.

Psycho burst into laughter

"Fuck what you talking about, Bruce, 'cause you don't know shit about that bitch," Psycho replied.

"Calm down, Psycho," Ryda said in a soothing voice as she rubbed his arm.

"No, fuck that!" he shouted as he snatched away from her. "I'm sick of muthafuckas giving that bitch a pass 'cause she's a dope head. I'm tired, Ryda." He slammed his fist on the coffee table, making the glass bowl bounce.

"Now look, Yajir, Psycho, or whatever the fuck you calling yo'self ..." Bruce started, pointing at Psycho.

I was staring at Psycho in shock. It seemed as if mentioning Sharie had struck a nerve in him. He was enraged. His veins in his neck and forehead were popped out, and his eyes held nothing but hatred.

"Naw, Bruce." He shook his head. "All the days and nights I went hungry; I'll give her a pass for that. Leaving me in the house alone for days; I'll give her a pass for that. But letting her many men come into our home and beat the shit out of me or try to molest me, I can't give her a pass for that. Addict or not, she should've protected me. She allowed it. Now tell me, Bruce, did I deserve that shit?"

Bruce and I both were standing there with our mouths hung open. We were speechless. I knew Sharie was an evil bitch, but to let her own son get harmed, I would have never thought that she would allow that. She seemed to be so loving when she was with him and J.B.

Bruce took a deep breath before speaking in a calm voice.

"No, Yajir, you didn't deserve that. I'm sorry that happened to you. Why didn't you tell me?"

"I only told Ryda. When she kicked me out, I put that shit behind me," he replied.

"Obviously not. Look how angry you are just mentioning her. It's evident that it still fucks with you," Bruce pointed out.

Ryda, laid her head on Psycho's shoulder as she wrapped her arms around his waist.

"I'm fine, Bruce. That bitch is dead to me. I don't give a fuck about her or what she let happen to me. I'm good; now drop the fucking subject." He hopped up off the couch and stormed out of the room.

"I'm sorry. He don't like talking about his childhood. I'ma go check on him; I'll be back," Ryda said in an apologetic tone before leaving the room.

I looked over at Bruce. He was sitting back in the chair, with his elbow resting on the arm of the chair and his chin resting on his fist, with a grim look on his face. I was still in disbelief. To think about grown ass men beating on that poor little boy, my heart was hurting for him. And I was secretly kicking myself for not checking on him throughout his life. Lord knows that I wanted to. I thought about him every time I thought about J.B., wondering how he was doing and if he were anything like his daddy.

"How could I not see that shit?" Bruce asked himself. His voice was slightly above a whisper, and sounded full of emotions.

"I don't think any of us would have seen Sharie allowing something like that to happen to Yajir," I assured.

I walked over to the side of the chair, sat on the arm, and laid my head on his shoulder. I was genuinely hurting. Hearing any child being abused tugged at my heartstrings. Being a victim of abuse myself, and knowing first-hand how it felt to be mistreated as a child gave me a full understanding of the emotional and mental scars that it leaves behind. You can forgive, move on, and let it go, but the truth in the matter is that pain never fully leaves you.

"Stephanie, had I known that was happening, Sharie and every last one of them niggas would've been sleeping with the devil," he assured.

"I know, Bruce." I ran my hand through his curly salt and pepper hair.

"Boy, J.B. is probably turning in his grave. I knew my man was resting in peace, but how can he, knowing his boy was going through that shit? I have it in mind to go over there and—" He paused.

"Bruce, stop it. Just stop it." I squeezed his hand. "If nobody else knows, I do," I added.

I met Bruce long before I met J.B., but it wasn't until J.B. and I had gotten together that me and Bruce got close. Bruce had a thing for me, but he was a lady's man, and I wouldn't give him the time of day. Besides that, I didn't want to bring no boys around my house and into the shit I was going through. But the night I'd told J.B. what was going on, it fucked his head up, and he vowed that he would take care of my problem. Not long after that, my uncle and his two buddies were found dead in an abandoned building. Police didn't care to investigate. To them, it was just three dead addicts in a building. Once I heard the news,

I went to J.B. and asked him about. He didn't confirm or deny; all he told me was that he'd take care of all my problems, and if he couldn't, Bruce would. That was all I needed to know.

A few minutes later, Psycho and Ryda came back downstairs, walking hand in hand. Bruce stood up and embraced Psycho.

"Bruce, man, you know—"

Bruce cut him off. "No apologies needed. I, on the other hand, owe you an apology," he said.

"Never that, Bruce. Never that. We good, man." Psycho gave Bruce dap and a brotherly hug.

"Aight, let's sit down and figure out how we gonna get you out of your current situation. If I got to lay some niggas down, consider it done. I'll always have yo' back," Bruce let him know.

Psycho nodded his head then sat down on the couch.
"Sunny, you talk to the girl?" he asked.

"I did, and she's down with it. She knows it's a risk, and I promised her that she would be nicely compensated."

After brainstorming ideas, with Bruce adding to them, we were able to come up with a full plan. Psycho said that Cutty would stay on alert until he felt that Psycho wasn't coming after him. With Bruce taking out some of his team, I didn't see that as being possible. Ryda thought that we should stick with her plan. She thought that if we got him to let his guard down, we could hit him easily, and the only way that he could do that was if he fell in love. At first, she wanted to be the girl that he fell for, but Psycho wasn't going for that shit. That was where I'd come in. Like I told them before, according to what Psycho said about Cutty, I had the perfect girl to put on him.

"When it comes to the bitches, you know I got that. Y'all just take care of the niggas," I suggested.

"Ok, and I got a few men in my corner that can keep eyes on him. Shit, if you want, they can rig shit up so that you can watch him from a distance," Bruce added.

"Like surveillance or some shit like that?" Psycho questioned.

"Hell yeah. That way, you can stay low and still make sure you know what the hell going on," Bruce replied.

"Yeah, and you can keep an eye on my girl too," I said.

Psycho sat with his back against the couch as if he were in deep thought.

"Aight, Bruce, do that. I need to stay low to make the nigga get comfortable." He nodded his head in agreement.

"I hope your girl move fast, Sunny, 'cause I'm ready to get this shit over with," Ryda stated.

"Patience is a virtue, my dear. Remember that. Cutty will get what's coming to him when the time is right. It may not be today, but trust me, it'll happen," Bruce avowed.

"Now, Yajir, how you looking on money? You got enough to hold you down for a while?" he asked.

"Yeah, I think. I hit a spot on my way home last night. I didn't count it yet, though," Psycho replied.

Ryda whipped her head around and looked at him with narrowed eyes. She folded her arms across her chest.

"So when was you gonna tell me that?" she inquired.

"Ryda, we will talk about that later. Chill out," Psycho told her.

Bruce shook his head. "Naw, Yajir, we don't need you doing that shit right now. You don't need no type of heat on you. Whatever you need, I got you."

"No, Bruce, I don't need you giving me no handouts. I'm a man; I can handle myself, and I can get my own money."

"Look, Yajir. Even a man needs help sometimes. The object here is to keep you out of harm's way. I wasn't there for you as a child, when I should've been, but I'm here now, and whatever you need, I got you. This ain't no handout or nothing. It's just what needs to happen."

After a brief testosterone-filled argument and a little convincing from Ryda, Psycho finally agreed to lay low and let Bruce help him.

"Now that everything is settled, I'ma get out of here," I said as I gave Ryda a hug.

"Let me walk you out," Bruce offered, and I agreed.

I walked over to Psycho and gave him a hug. "I'll bring my girl by to meet you so we can brief her on her mark."

"Aight. Remember, he loves a certain type of woman," he reminded.

"Psycho, I have a memory like and elephant. I got this. Just take care of yo'self and my lil' mini me here. Let the O.G.' s handle the basics. Just be ready to kill that nigga, Cutty," I said before giving him another hug and a kiss on the cheek.

As Bruce and I were headed to my car, he told me that he knew that I was one of Panama's girls. I wasn't surprised. Panama and his girls were known in the streets.

"Yeah, Bruce, I was, but now, I'm running his shit," I confirmed.

"So is that where you met Yajir? Was he one of your clients?" he questioned.

I wasn't going to tell him all of Ryda's business, so I gave him the short version. "No, I met Ryda, not him. I was working the block one night and saw a young, homeless girl. I helped her get on her feet, same as J.B. did me. That's it in a nut shell."

Bruce gave me a questionable look then pulled me into and embrace. "I'm sorry I wasn't there to stop you from getting involved with Panama. I should've came and took you out of that place." He pulled away from me, and stroked my hair. "You're too damn beautiful." He kissed my cheek then opened my car door for me.

"Bruce, we both was fucked up when J.B. died, and in spite of everything, I had a good life. But thank you."

He gave me a wink, then closed my door. As he was headed to his car, I laid my head against the seat and closed my eyes.

"J.B., I know you're up there. Please watch over us and protect us as we guide your son through this shit. And I promise I'll do all I can to protect him," I prayed.

CUTTY

"Oww, Cutty, slow down! You're hurting me, and my legs are tired," Renee complained as I pounded the hell out of her pussy.

This shit with Yajir had me in a fucked up mood, and I needed some way to rid myself of my frustrations.

"Bitch, shut the fuck up, and keep yo' muthafuckin' legs up and open so I can get this nut." I grimaced.   I placed my hand around her neck, choking her just a little, as I continued roughly plowing into her.

"Ahh, ahh, ahh!" she screamed loudly with a distorted look on her face as she started turning red.

I didn't give a fuck if I was hurting her or not. She was getting and taking all this dick and pain. I flipped her ass around, buried her face in the pillow, and continued beating the shit out of her pussy. You know the saying 'face down ass up?' Yeah, I went in hard and deep, causing the bitch to scream for God's mercy.

"Cutty, please," she begged.

That shit fell on deaf ears. She had no choice but to let me take my pinned-up aggressions out on her. If the bitch didn't want the dick, then she shouldn't have called in the first place.

After about another fifteen to twenty minutes of hair-pulling, ass-slapping, rough sex, I took the condom off so I could bust all over her back and ass and felt a small hint of relief. I grabbed my t-shirt and wiped the dripping nut off my rod and off her back. I didn't trust bitches, she might try to do that turkey basting shit, and I ain't tryna have no unwanted seeds running around here. I tossed my shirt in the hamper in the bathroom then hopped my ass in the shower.

When I got back in my room, shorty was balled up in my bed, under the cover, knocked the hell out. I stood at the foot of my bed, looking down at her, thinking this bitch done lost her damn mind.

"Get the fuck up," I demanded, mushing her head into the pillow.

She jumped up, looking around with her eyes all wide and holding the cover against her bare breast.

"What the fuck, Cutty? What's wrong with you?" she questioned, looking confused.

"Get yo' funky ass out my bed! Go the fuck home!" I barked.

"For real, Cutty? This how you doing me?" she asked as she slid out of the bed.

"Bitch, you ain't special. I treat you the same way I treat all the other hoes out there. Now hurry the fuck up. I got shit to do," I said, getting my stash to roll a blunt.

Renee rolled her eyes then started grabbing her clothes as she scurried around my room, talking shit. I didn't give a fuck about what she was saying. She served her purpose, and now, it was time for her to make her exit.

"Bye, asshole!" she spat as she walked out of my door, slamming it behind her.

I laughed at her ass as I headed to the door and locked it. I went to the kitchen and grabbed a bottle of Don Julio Tequila then walked back to the living room.

As I was making myself comfortable on the couch, my phone started ringing. I looked at the screen and saw Kayo's name flash across the screen. I snatched my phone off the table, eager to here word on Yajir.

"Talk," I answered.

"Yo, Cutty, man. I don't know what happened, but I had eyes on Yajir. He was in his apartment. I watched him for—"

I had to cut that rambling ass muthafucka off. "Kayo, get to the fucking point. What the fuck are you telling me?"

"I fell asleep in the car, and when I woke up, his apartment was pitch black, and he was nowhere in sight. "

"What? You fell asleep? What type of bullshit am I hearing? Do I have a bunch of imbeciles working for me or what? For real, what the fuck do I pay you incompetent assholes for?"

"Cutty, I'm sorry. I wasn't prepared to sit at the nigga's crib all night. I'd been running around all day tryna find his ass to make up for last night," he explained.

I didn't want to hear none of his excuses. I gave his ass a simple job to do, and I expected for him to do the shit.

"Kayo, I don't give a fuck if you tired, hungry, or need to take a shit—you keep yo' ass at that nigga's crib until I know what the fuck he's doing, or yo' ass will be on my hit list." I hung up the phone.

Grabbing my bottle, I was enraged. *This dumbass nigga, fell asleep,* I thought as I took a big swig. After facing the whole jay and putting a big ass dent in that bottle of Don Julio, I was fucked up, and thoughts of how Yajir and I used to get into petty little fights came flooding my mind.

"Where the fuck you think you going with my shit, Cutty?"

"Nigga, it's a fucking jacket. Can't a nigga borrow the bitch?"

"Naw, I just copped that. Hell no, you ain't borrowing it. Shit you don't know how to return things."

"Man, fuck that, Yajir. You knew damn well that I wanted this jacket. You didn't even know the shit existed until I showed it to you. You had to be the first to get it, right?"

"Cutty, you crazy. You always on that, who gets it first, bullshit. Nigga, I did what I had to do to get it. You want everything handed to you. You want easy money. Shit ain't always easy. Sometimes, you got to put in work."

"So sticking niggas up is work? That's not easy money? Fuck you, Yajir. I'ma show you how to make that easy money—watch. You think you the shit 'cause J.B. your daddy?"

"Leave my daddy out of this. You wanna be a dope boy? Do that then. I ain't got shit to do with that. But that jacket—that's mine, so you can put it right back where you got it from."

"Fuck you and yo' stolen ass jacket." Pthu!

"Nigga, did you just spit on my got damn jacket? I should split yo' shit." Whap!

"Nigga!"

Whap! Whap! Umph! Whap! Whap!

"Get the fuck off me, nigga."

"Get the fuck up, and get the fuck out my house before I really beat yo' ass."

"Man, fuck you, Yajir!"

Yajir and I used to fight like shit, but that fight was the last fight that nigga and I had. We were fourteen then. He always thought he was tough and could beat me, but shit changed. We were grown ass men, and I handled shit on a whole other level.

"Yeah, Yajir, you always had to compete with me. Always had to have what I had. I showed yo' ass, though. I make paper. You still broke and robbing muthafuckas. I was gonna elevate yo' game and help you get that bag, but yo' dumbass wanna lie to me. And now, you wanna start a beef with me. I got something for you, though. I'll handle yo' bitch ass myself. Shit ain't the same as it used to be. You ain't gonna win this war, nigga; I put that on everything."

Laughing at my own thoughts, I picked up the phone to make the call that I really needed to make. It was time for me to let Yajir know that this was not a game. His ass was dead on site.

PSYCHO

Stretched out on the bed with my Beats on, my legs crossed at the ankles, and one arm tucked under my head, I hit shuffle on my iPod then lit the blunt that was hanging out of my mouth. I closed my eyes and let the music and smoke take me to another world. I'd been secretly beating myself up all day for telling Bruce and Sunny the truth about my childhood. With the expception of Ryda,I intended on taking that shit to the grave with me.But it was something about the way Bruce was basically demanding that I give that bitch respect all because she gave birth to me, that pissed me the hell off.

Shit, any woman can give birth, but not every woman deserves to have a child. I know that seems like a fucked up thing to say, but shit, that's the fucking truth. Some women don't know shit about raising a fucking kid, and Sharie Jordan was one of them. She should've swallowed me, spit me out, or something—anything but had me. And after knowing that my daddy left Sunny for that bitch, I think the only reason why she had me was to keep him.

From the stories that Bruce and others told me about my daddy, he was the man, and Sharie was treated like a ghetto queen or something just for being his girl. That was until she stopped sucking his dick and started sucking on that glass dick. From the pictures that I'd seen of my mother from back then, she was fine as fuck and had a body any nigga would've loved to bust a nut in. I know that's some sick shit to say about my moms, but shit, I speak facts. She was definitely something nice to have on your arm, but now the bitch looked like the walking dead. She didn't look nothing like the woman in those pictures that complemented my daddy so well. I'm talking about no ass, missing teeth, nappy ass hair, and she looked like she didn't know the meaning of soap and water. I didn't see how niggas still wanted to slide up in her. I guess, the commercial with an egg being fried that says *this is your brain on drugs* was on point 'cause the niggas that stuck dick up in her brains must be fried.

"Baby, you okay?" Ryda asked, removing the Beats from my head as she climbed on top of me, wearing nothing but her little ass night gown.

I adjusted myself on the bed so that we could both be comfortable then put my blunt in the ashtray.

"Yeah, I'm good. Just thinking. That's all," I replied.

"What you thinking about?" she inquired.

"Shit, a lot of shit," I answered.

She folded her arms across her chest and looked at me with raised brows and pursed lips, wanting me to elaborate on my answer. I laughed as I scooted up a little on the bed, almost making her fall off me.

"I was thinking about my parents and the shit that happened today. I can't believe I told Bruce and Sunny that shit."

"Honestly, Psycho, maybe it was time. Maybe by letting it out, you can really put it behind you and start to heal."

"What about you? When you gonna put yo' past behind you and heal?" I asked, reminding her that she wasn't nowhere near over her shit.

"When there's nothing left to be done but sit back and enjoy my life with the man that I love," she replied with a smirk on her face.

"You can sit back and enjoy me now. You love me, right? You my Ryda forever, right?"

Placing my face in her hands, she lifted my head and kissed me passionately.

"Of course, I enjoy my life with you, and yes, I love you. I'm your Ryda forever. But I cannot fully enjoy my life, knowing muthafuckas are out there happy when they don't deserve an ounce of happiness in their lives."

I scooted up into a sitting position and grabbed her by the back of her head, pulling her closer and kissing her.

"Revenge tastes so sweet coming from your lips," I said.

She flashed me a devilish grin as she started grinding on me, making my manhood stand at attention.

"Your lips not the only sweetness I want to taste," I teased as I laid back and began to lift her to place her on my face so I could taste that sweet nectar between her thighs.

Before I could get her perfectly positioned where I wanted her, the ringing of my phone interrupted us. Ryda teasingly stuck her tongue out at me as she quickly reached for my phone from the bed, beside me. She was saved by the bell, and she knew it. I was about to have myself a nice feast on her pussy, making her ass scream and beg for mercy, knowing good and hell well that I wasn't about to show her none.

Ryda picked up my phone and looked at the screen.

"It's an unknown number," she said, looking at me suspiciously.

"Man, fuck that. I don't know who the fuck that is." I tried pulling her upwards, but she pulled away.

"Naw, Psycho, you gonna answer that damn phone, right here, right now," she commanded with a hint of attitude in her tone.

I chuckled. "Trust me. It ain't no girl," I assured, already knowing what she was thinking.

She passed me the phone. "Then answer it," she demanded.

Shaking my head, I took the phone out of her hand then hit the accept button. "Yeah, who dis?" I barked into the phone.

"I know we wasn't exactly what some might call boys, but I thought we was better than this."

Even though his words were slurred, and his voice sounded a little too high pitched, I knew exactly who it was.   "Cutty?"

"Yeah, you know who the fuck this is, muthafucka. I really wasn't tryna start no beef with you, but you came after me."

"Nigga, fuck you talking about? You had niggas hit my crib. You started this shit, but I'm damn sure 'nuff gonna finish it!" I shouted into the phone.

"Keep shit a hunnid. You been hatin' on me yo' whole sorry ass life, nigga. You can't stand that I came up, and you didn't!" he yelled.

I looked at the phone with a scrunched face, trying to figure out what the hell this nigga was talking about. I ain't never in my life hated on this muthafucka. The way I saw it, the nigga was always hating on me. For what reason? I didn't know.

"Cutty, fuck all that dumb shit you spitting right now. This yo' shit. You got beef with me? Handle that shit like a fucking man 'cause I'm down for whatever."

"Nigga, fuck you! You just signed yo' death certificate. Come get me, bitch."

The line went dead.

"Is that a threat, bitch? Huh? Is that a muthafuckin' threat?" I yelled into the dead phone line before throwing it at the wall.

"Nigga, you called me, threatening me? I got something for yo' ass! Ain't no bitch in me, muthafucka, but I can show you better than tell you, bitch ass nigga. You must be scared, fucking coward ass muthafucka!" I raged as a stomped around the room, putting on my clothes.

"Psycho, wait! Stop," Ryda franticly spoke as she jumped in my way, pushing and pulling on me, trying to stop me.

I pushed her to the side several times, but she continued jumping in my face and getting in my way. That shit was pissing me off even more.

"Ryda, get the fuck off me. The nigga told me to come and get him, and that's what the fuck I'm about to do," I fumed as I grabbed my gun and some bullets out of the drawer.

"No, you not, Psycho. That's what he wants. We got to stick to our plans," she spoke with desperation in her voice.

"Fuck that plan. That nigga got a death wish, and I'm the nigga that's gonna make that shit come true," I snapped as I headed towards the bedroom door.

Ryda jumped in front of the door, slamming it shut. "No, you can't do this, Psycho. I won't let you." She placed her hands on my chest, shoving me away from the door.

"Ryda, move!" I yelled.

She shook her head no. I tried pushing her away from me, but she held on to my shirt.

"Ryda, for real, get the fuck off me. I don't want to hurt you, but if you don't get the fuck out of my way, I swear I will—"

"You will what? Hurt me, huh? Is that what you'll do, Psycho? Well, I don't give a fuck. If that's what the hell you have to do, then do it 'cause I'll be damned if I let you leave this house and get yourself killed!" she shouted, getting up in my face.

I was enraged as I stood there, staring at her, with my fists balled tight. My blood was boiling, and I could feel tiny beads of sweat forming on my nose. The veins in my arms were bulging out from how hard I was holding my fist. My heart was pounding, and my breathing was heavy. The more I stared at Ryda, the angrier I became.

"Don't make me hurt you, Ryda, please. I don't want to. I need you to get the fuck out of my way. Now," I spoke through clenched teeth as I tried to fight the anger that I had towards her.

She shook her head no. "Don't you see what he's doing? He is taunting you. He wants you to make a stupid ass mistake like this. I can't let you fall for his trap. This is clearly a fucking set up, Psycho. Calm the hell down and listen to me, please. You don't know what he got waiting for you. You cannot go blindly. Now, you told me that he's not the nigga you can just run up on; you have to be careful. Let him think you a bitch. Let him think you hiding from him. I don't give a fuck. We got a plan, and we have to stick to it, baby, please." Her eyes started to well up, and her voice was thick with emotion as she continued speaking. "Please, don't go. Please, just calm down and be smart about this. If you don't listen to me ever again, please, baby, listen to me now. I need you to do this for me, Psycho. If you love me, stay with me."

The tears that were pouring out her eyes as she pleaded with me tugged at my heart. This girl truly loved me, and any questions or doubt that I may have had before, disappeared at that moment. She was standing with her back against the door and her arms stretch across the frame with a look of fear on her tear-filled face. She was determined not to let me leave.

A feeling of warmth shot through my body as my breathing started to become relaxed. I closed my eyes and took several deep breaths, trying to get my pounding heart to relax as well.

"Ryda," I called in a hushed tone.

"No, Psycho. I'm not letting you go," she sobbed.

I opened my eyes and saw the hurt in hers. "I do love you. I'll stay," I said.

She exhaled the breath that she was holding before throwing herself in my arms. "Thank you," she whispered repeatedly as she kissed me all over my face.

With one arm wrapped around her waist and her dangling from my neck, I walked her over to the bed, and sat her down. I took the gun out of the small of my back then placed it and the bullets back inside the drawer to assure her that I was staying. I sat on the side of the bed and ran my hands down my face.

"I can't believe this nigga had the balls to call me talking shit like I'm a fucking punk or something. He must be out of his fucking mind."

"Don't worry about that shit, baby. He gonna get his. I promise."

I got up from the bed, removed my clothes, then flopped back down on the bed. Ryda grabbed my blunt out of the ashtray, lit it, and then climbed on top of me, straddling me.

"Can I get high with you?" she asked as she took a toke of the jay.

I looked at her like she was crazy. She knew damn well she couldn't handle no damn weed. She started coughing, and I laughed at her for faking like she be chiefing. I took the blunt out of her hand, took a long pull, and let that shit marinate then blew it out slowly. I instantly started to feel some relief. I took several more puffs of the jay and became fully relaxed.

"Come on, Psycho. Stop being a hoover." She reached for the blunt. "I told you I wanna get high with you," she whined.

I held the blunt high over my head so that she couldn't reach it.

"You think you can handle smoking this while I finish the meal I was about to eat a minute ago?" I asked.

Without saying a word, she crawled up towards my face and took the blunt out of my hand then put it to her lips. That was the only answer I needed. I grabbed her by the waist, pulling her up on my face, giving myself full access to her already wet honey pot. I went all in. A few seconds of my tongue swirling around her clit was all it took for her to put the blunt down in the astray, letting it burn out.

Around an hour and a half later, Ryda was sprawled across the bed, knocked the fuck out. I wore her ass out. She wouldn't let me go handle Cutty's bitch ass, so I had to make her pay for that shit. I made her bust so many times that she damn near passed out. But as she laid beside me, peacefully sleeping, and snoring like shit, I couldn't get that phone call from that nigga out of my mind. Careful not to wake her, I slid out of bed, grabbed my all black, my gun, and bullets out of the drawer then tiptoed out of the room. I slowly, and with ease, crept down the steps. I quickly threw on my clothes and shoes then quietly exited the house.

Heading down Highway 240 West, I checked the time to make sure that I was on schedule with Cutty. It was a little after midnight, which meant he was just getting home and getting ready to unwind. As I continued to drive, I started to think about that phone call again. Cutty was already drunk, so maybe he wasn't home.

Where the fuck you at? I wondered as I searched my brain for the answer. I'd been around Cutty and knew him well enough to be able to predict his next move. He made that threatening phone call to me. Ain't no way in hell he would go home, knowing that I knew his routine. He was probably at the house he had on Florida Street. That was his stash spot, not for his products, but that was where he went to keep people from knowing where he really laid his head—usually bitches that he fucked and had no intentions on entertaining again.

Taking exit 28B, towards S Parkway, I used one hand to make sure my gun was fully loaded.

Death is coming for you, nigga, I thought as I turned off my lights and pulled on to his street. I pulled into a dark area between houses then shut my engine off. I got out of the car and was getting ready to start walking towards his house when I heard voices. I peeked around the wall.

"What the fuck?" I mumbled to myself.

Cutty was coming out of his house with three niggas, dressed in all black, like they were ready to go do dirt.

"Oh, it's like that?" I questioned, chuckling to myself as I watched them climb in the truck then pull out of the drive way.

I crouched down so they couldn't see me as I eased into my car as they drove right by me. The truck reached the end of the street, and I started my engine. Once they turned off his street, I waited for a few cars to pass by before turning off the street, following behind them. Making sure to keep a good distance, I followed those niggas all the way from his house to my apartment.

"Ain't this some funny ass shit?" I asked myself as Cutty pulled next to a car that was sitting outside of my apartment building.

I parked my car in the next court then headed around the back of the buildings, making sure to stay out of sight. Crouching down, I planted my back against the wall of the building next to mine and slowly made my way to the row of uncut bushes that were in between that building and mine. The way the bushes were set up, they would completely block me from their view. It was the perfect spot to hide.

"Cutty, man, I swear that nigga, Yajir, must have dipped. His scary ass." Kayo chuckled.

"Yeah, that bitch got that nigga's nose open. Got that nigga thinking he go hard. I should take his bitch. You said she got a fat ass and big ass titties, right?" Cutty asked, snickering.

I felt my temperature starting to rise at the mentioning of Ryda. I had to coach myself in my head to calm down. I wanted to jump out of them bushes and peel the niggas' wigs back for calling Ryda out of her name and talking about her fucking body.

"Yeah, she's fat as fuck. I don't know how she hooked up with his ass." Kayo shook his head.

Cutty stood silent for a second as if he was thinking.

"Fuck this nigga at?" Cutty shouted.

"Man, fuck him. I told you, the nigga probably dipped. We can run up in his shit and see if the nigga's shit in there. If it is, then we know he'll be back, and we can continue to keep eyes on his bitch ass," Kayo suggested.

These niggas really think I'm a bitch, I thought, holding in my laugh.

"Aight, let's do that. Maybe we can find out where the nigga at," Cutty replied before they headed into the building.

I was glad that I took all our important shit with me when I came to get some of our things, so I knew these niggas wouldn't find shit on or about Ryda and me. Also, I was glad that I left a bunch of clothes and shit in the closets and drawers. Now these niggas would think that I was coming back, and trust me, I would, but they wouldn't see me coming.

"Okay, Kayo, you just made yo'self my first target," I mumbled to myself as dipped back into the darkness and headed back to my car.

"I got to tell Bruce this shit here. These muthafuckas is watching my crib like they the police." I chuckled. I picked up the phone and was about to call Bruce, but then, I thought that it was too damn late to call his ass. "I'll holler at him tomorrow," I said, tossing the phone on the seat. I cranked up the volume on the radio then rolled down my window to get some fresh air as I made the twenty-minute drive back to the house.

Before entering the neighborhood, I turned the music off so that I didn't draw any unnecessary attention from the neighbors. I slowly approached the gate, punched in the security code, and waited for the gates to open. I made my way up the circle driveway. Grabbing my gun, bullets, and my phone off the seat, I placed them all in my pockets then headed up to the door. Putting the key in the lock, I slowly turned it and the door knob at the same time. I went inside and slowly closed and locked the door. It was dark as hell in the house. I couldn't see shit but the key pad for the alarm. I used the wall to guide me to the key pad and turned the alarm on then took off my shoes. Feeling around blindly, I finally reached the rail to the stairs.

"Where the fuck you been?" Ryda asked from the top of the stairs as she flicked on the light.

RYDA

Psycho looked like a deer that got caught in headlights as he stood silent at the bottom of the steps, wide-eyed, with a look of shock plastered on his face. He wasn't expecting me to be sitting on the top step, in the dark, waiting for him to sneak his ass back in the house.

"Answer my fucking question. Where the fuck you been?" I repeated.

He bit down on his bottom lip as he took in a deep breath then exhaled it. "Baby, look. Don't be mad. Everything is ok," he answered.

I looked at him like he was crazy as I shook my head and let out an angry chuckle. "Mad ain't even the word to explain how I feel right now. I asked you a fucking question. Now answer it," I demanded.

I already knew the answer, but I wanted to see if he would tell me the truth. The scowl on my face must have told him that there was no way around answering the question. With defeat written all over his face, Psycho exhaled deeply before answering.

"Nothing happened, I swear. I didn't do nothing dumb," he explained, slowly walking up the steps.

"No, Psycho, you did do something dumb. Leaving this house after you said you'd stay was dumb. What if something happened to you, and I'm home sleeping and not knowing shit? Did you think about that?" I paused before continuing, "Never mind. Don't bother to answer. It's obvious that you didn't."

I quickly got up from the steps and marched into the bedroom. Psycho rushed up the steps, calling my name, and trying to get my attention. I ignored him. The truth was that I was more hurt than I was angry. I felt like he played me. He calmed down just enough for me to let my guard down; then, he fucked me until I was exhausted and passed out. Then, he snuck out of the house like some dumb ass nigga sneaking away from his side bitch. The moment I woke up and realized he was gone, I felt like the trust I had in him went out the door with him.

"Baby, listen to me," he began, but I cut him off.

"Why should I, when you lied to me? How can I trust anything you say right now? I got up to get something to drink, only to find out you were gone. You left this house without making a sound, so you sneaking around now?"

"Ryda, I didn't lie. I had no intentions on leaving this house tonight, but—"

"Bullshit, Psycho! You stood in that very same spot and said that you love me, and you'll stay. Only to turn around and do the exact opposite. So how can you stand there now and tell me that damn lie? You had no intentions. You full of shit right now."

"So I'm a liar now? I'm full of shit? Yes, I did leave and go after Cutty, but like I said, I didn't intend on doing that. I was lying beside you, listening to you sleeping peacefully, while my mind was going a mile a minute, thinking about the shit that nigga said on the phone. I got mad, and I wanted to put an end to this shit. So yes, I went after him, and I'm glad I did 'cause I found out some shit we needed to know."

"Good, then be glad. I'm going to bed. Sunny is bringing the girl over in the morning." I snatched the cover back then climbed in bed.

"So you don't want to know what I found out?" he asked, looking at me, confused.

"No, I'm going to bed," I snapped as I snatched the cover over my head.

I was upset, and didn't want to hear nothing else he had to say at that moment. A few minutes later, I felt Psycho get in the bed. He tried to wrap his arm around me, but I kindly and politely moved his arm from me and placed it back on his side.

"Oh, it's like that?" he snickered.

I moved away from him as I drew an imaginary line in the cover, in between us, letting him know that I didn't want him to touch me.

"Yeah, it's like that." I turned my back on him, pulled the cover over my head, and rocked myself to sleep.

The next morning, I woke up still pissed at Psycho, but instead of being petty and making his ass starve like I wanted to, I decided to carry on with my usual routine. I hopped in the shower then went downstairs to cook him breakfast. First thing Psycho did in the morning, after washing up and brushing his teeth, was smoke a blunt. That usually made him hungry as hell. I decided to cook blueberry waffles, eggs, bacon, sausage, bagels, and fruit salad. As I was placing the eggs on our plates, Psycho came in the kitchen, smoking his blunt.

"Damn, baby, it smells good as shit in here. You must not be mad at a nigga no more. I thought I was gonna have to fend for myself this morning," he stated jokingly.

I didn't respond. I continued fixing our plates as if he weren't even standing there.

"So you not talking to me?" he inquired.

Tuning him out, and just to let him know that I was still pissed, I rolled my eyes at him as I continued moving around the kitchen. Psycho stood silently, leaning against the island, smoking his blunt, and eyeing me suspiciously.

"You real funny." He chuckled, shaking his head.

After placing our plates on the table, I headed to the refrigerator to get the juice. Psycho yanked me by my arm and pulled me close to him, wrapping both of his arms around my waist to hold me in place.

"Keep playing with me, and I'ma bend yo' ass over this counter and knock that that attitude right out of you." He leaned in to kiss me.

I grabbed his lips squeezing them a little. "That won't work," I stated.

"Oh, yeah?" He snickered as he walked me to the counter across from us and turned me around.

"Get off!" I shouted, trying to turn around.

Using one hand to push me down on the counter and the other to hold me around my waist, Psycho pressed his manhood against me. He leaned on top of me and started sucking on my ear as he slid his hand up my shirt.

"What won't work?" he asked, fondling my breast and sucking my neck.

My body started to betray me as the tingling sensations shot through my body, causing my juices to flow down below.

"Mmm." I moaned, throwing my head back against his chest.

He took my arms and placed them around his neck, then continued sucking on my neck and ear as his hands continued exploring my body.

"Tell me you want me," he commanded in a seductive voice.

Biting then sucking my bottom lip, I close my eyes and gave in to his command.

"I want you," I whispered.

Psycho turned me around, placed me on the counter, and then started kissing up my thigh. I opened my legs to give him full access to my already throbbing box. As he got closer to my pleasure zone, I became anxious to feel his thick tongue swirling around my wetness. Leaning my head back against the cabinet, I closed my eyes, waiting for Psycho to pleasure me. I didn't know if it were the anticipation or my eagerness to feel his tongue, but it was taking Psycho forever to get to my spot. I reached down to pull his head upward, but he wasn't there. I quickly popped open my eyes to see him leaning against the island, watching me, with a smirk on his face.

"Now that I got yo' attention, we can talk." He chortled.

Looking at him like he must have lost him mind, my eyes drifted to the gap between his sweats shorts and his stomach; then, they moved down to his erection.

"You and him can have a conversation later. Right now, me and you need to talk," he said, folding his arms across his chest.

Folding my arms across my chest as well, I rolled my eyes to let him know that I still had an attitude. What I couldn't let him know was the attitude was now because he got me all hot and bothered only to leave me wet and horny.

"What we need to talk about? You sneaking out last night? I already told you I don't want to hear shit you got to say."

"Well, that's too damn bad 'cause I got something to say, and you gonna sit yo' lil' ass right there and listen."

Who in the hell do he think he is? I thought. He must've thought that I was really gonna let him tell me what the hell I was gonna listen to. I chuckled before hopping off the counter. Psycho scooped me up with one arm and placed me back on the counter.

"Don't play games with me, Ryda. I told yo' ass to sit right there and listen to what I had to say, and that's what the fuck you gonna do. You wanna try me, go ahead 'cause I can do this shit all day."

The seriousness in his eyes and tone let me know that he wasn't playing with my ass, so I decided not to try him again. I huffed then folded my arms across my chest, pouting.

"Go ahead. Talk," I instructed.

He blank-stared me for a second then shook his head.

"I'm sorry. I shouldn't have left. You can either forgive me or not, but me leaving was worth it. Cutty got niggas camped out at our apartment, keeping eyes on us. Like this nigga got these goofy ass muthafuckas doing a real live stake out."

I couldn't believe what I was hearing. This nigga Cutty had to be out of his damn mind. I had to be sure I was hearing what Psycho was saying. This clown had us under surveillance and shit.

"What?" I asked with a twisted up face.

"Yeah, this nigga got eyes on us, so he thinks. I saw the shit with my own eyes. I followed the nigga from his crib to ours. He had Kayo and Cliff already there, sitting outside our building."

I let out a deep belly laugh, not sure if the shit was funny or just so unbelievable that it was nothing to do but laugh. Psycho looked at me confused before he burst into laughter, and just like that, my anger towards him disappeared. The sounds of the doorbell interrupted our laughter.

"Oh shit, it's Sunny. I told you last night that she was bringing the girl over here so we could prep her, right?" I asked, hopping of the counter.

"You mentioned something like that," he replied as I rushed to answer the door.

****

"You got to turn heads when you walk in the room, but at the same time, you don't want it to appear like you're trying to draw attention," Sunny explained to Kesha.

Kesha was the girl Sunny chose to go after Cutty. She looked like a younger Nia Long—bowlegs and all. In fact, she was the spitting image of Nia Long when she played Debbie in the movie *Friday*; the only difference was Kesha had bigger breast, hips, and ass than Nia Long. Psycho said that she was the perfect choice, because Cutty had had a crush on Nia Long ever since that movie.

We were training Kesha on the girlfriend experience. It's the term used when one of our clients wanted us to engage in reciprocal sexual pleasure with a little more intimacy and less focus on just having sex. Only a handful of girls at The House of Angels did the girlfriend experience. I was the best girl for the job. I had no feelings, so I never worried about catching any.

"Ryda, show her the walk," Sunny instructed.

I got up from the couch and strutted across the floor with my head up and shoulders back, leading with my breast as I let my arms swing loosely, back and forth, and my hips swiveled from side to side.

"Now, you try it," I suggested.

Kesha stood tall with her head held high then started strutting across the floor.

"That's right. Put more weight on your heels. Let your arms swing more natural. Come on. Shoulders, hips, heels," I coached.

"That's great, Kesha. Keep practicing, and you'll be more comfortable with the alignment of your body and the movements. Honey, let me tell you, that walk sends a message saying that you are in control of yo' body, and that you are confident in yo'self. Niggas love that shit," Sunny boasted.

I nodded my head in agreement. "You'll be surprised at how many niggas approach you."

"It's so many little things you can do to make a nigga think you the shit," Sunny stated grabbing her body guard's Biggs hand, then leading him to the couch.

She sat him down then pulled the ottoman closer to him.

"Your body speak in volumes," Sunny said as she sat on the ottoman across from Biggs.

"Remember, men love to see your leg length, so show them in any way can," she told her demistrating how to sit with your legs crossed sideways. "And always gaze into his eyes," I added leaning over Sunny's shoulders to show her how to gaze seductively.

Sunny started to explain how to stroke his ego with your body language. Suddenly, Psycho jumped out of his seat with a scowl on his face.

"Y'all been at this shit for hours. Don't y'all think that's enough hoe training for one day!" he shouted.

Sunny and I both stared at him in disbelief. I was highly offended by his comment. It was like he called me a hoe, once again. I felt insulted, and I was pissed.

"Hoe training? Did you really just say hoe training?" I asked in disbelief.

"You heard what the fuck I said, Ryda. Hoe. Training. Is this the type of shit you do?" He looked over at Sunny. "This what you did for Ryda? You trained her like that too?" he tittered as he shook his head and looked me dead in the eyes

"The girlfriend experience, huh? Well Sunny, pat yo'self on the back 'cause you teaches real well." He stormed out of the room and out of the back door.

I started to go after him, but Sunny stopped me.

"No, Ryda, let me go," she offered, then walked out of the room.

Exhaling deeply as I ran my hands across the top of my head, I sat down on the couch. I couldn't believe his ungrateful ass.

SUNNY

After Psycho's little blow up, I followed him to the backyard, where he was sitting on the lounger with his head resting on the back and running his hands down his face. I sat down beside him. For a moment, we sat in silence, staring at each other. I could see so much pain and anger in his eyes, and it was breaking my heart. I placed my hand on his.

"You wanna tell me what that was about in there?" I asked.

"No, not really," he replied, getting up and walking over to the bar.

He grabbed a bottle of beer out of the mini fridge then sat on the bar stool.

"Psycho, come back over here, please," I demanded.

Psycho's face held no expression as he glared at me for a while before getting up and coming to sit back down.

"What's up, Psycho? I know there's something in your head that caused you to get upset. Talk to me," I insisted.

Chugging down his beer, Psycho shook his head as he closed his eyes. I thought for a second that I was gonna have to damn near beg his ass to get him to talk, but I was wrong. As soon as he swallowed that last sip of beer, he looked at me and shook his head. Then, he began speaking.

"I don't know what's wrong with me, Sunny. I just get so crazy over her, and sometimes it's hard as hell to trust her after knowing what she used to do. It's like I'm waiting for her to fuck around on me like Sharie use to do to my daddy. I use to see them sometimes, kissing and just being real affectionate towards each other, like they were truly in love. Then, when he wasn't home, Sharie would have other niggas over, getting high, and I would catch her fucking or sucking them niggas. Now, meeting you and finding out he loved you but cheated with Sharie—it's like what the fuck is this shit all for? If you love somebody, why the hell do you fuck around on them? This shit is complicated as hell."

"No, honey, love is not complicated. People make it that way." I took his hand in mine before continuing. "Psycho, you can't base your relationship with Ryda on the shit you seen your mother do or what I told you about my and your father's relationship. We were all fucked up ass people, and we did a lot of fucked up shit. You and Ryda have your own bond and your own reasons why you love each other."

"Yeah, Sunny, but we are some fucked up ass people, too. So, how can we keep our shit tight when we got so much shit inside that fucks with us?"

"By trusting each other, learning to communicate with each other, and most of all, continuing to love one another. That's all you have to do. Things are not gonna always be peaches and cream. Shit tends to get a little rough, but how you get through the rough patches speaks volumes about your relationship. You and Ryda are young, and young love is a bitch. Trust me, I know. I also know that the short period of time that

I've known Ryda, I've never seen her smile so much. You make her happy. My advice to you is to trust her whole heartily and stop letting her past be a factor in your relationship. Now, put your grown man drawers on, get your ass in there, and apologize for insulting her and Kesha. Then, let's finish this shit so we can all get on with our lives."

"Thanks, Sunny, and I apologize for snapping at you, and for insulting you as well." He pulled me into and embrace.

"Boy, I'm good. And if J.B. was here, he would've knocked yo' head clean off your shoulders for acting like that." I chuckled.

"You don't know how much I would love for him to be here to do that." He snickered.

"Yes, I do. I would love for him to be here, too." I kissed his cheek then got up from the lounger, pulling him up with me. As we were walking back in the house, Bruce was coming through the kitchen, heading out back where we were.

"Damn, Stephanie, you get finer every time I see you!" he exclaimed as he gave me the once over.

"Hello, Bruce," I greeted as I gave him a hug.

"And you smell good, too. I don't know how in the hell I'm gonna be able to focus on the task at hand with you looking all good and smelling like heaven," he said as he held me tighter.

"Flirt on your own time, old man. We got shit to do," Psycho blurted out.

"Shit, this old man will kick yo' lil' young ass. You better watch that tone," Bruce spoke in a serious tone. "Now, we know that Cutty got niggas watching yo' house like you under police surveillance. Well, I got something for Cutty. Let me show you how ole Bruce get down," he added, leading us to the living room.

Ryda's gaze was icy cold as she gave Psycho the side eye. I shook my head, laughing. From the look in her eyes, I knew that an apology wasn't gonna be enough to get Psycho out of the dog house.

"Look like you got some serious begging to do," I stated as I nudged Psycho towards Ryda.

After Psycho apologized to both Ryda and Kesha, we sat down with Bruce so he could explain all the gadgets he had in his bags. I couldn't begin to explain all that high tech shit that Bruce had; the only thing I knew was he'd given Kesha a gold, heart-shaped pendant to wear on a gold chain with a gold-band bracelet to go along with it. He explained that both pieces of jewelry had built in cameras. The necklace allowed us to see what was in front of her, while the bracelet let us see what was behind her. He said he needed to see everything from every angle to ensure her safety. He also planned on having someone around her at all times, in case she got into trouble. I didn't know where the fuck Bruce got this shit from, but I was sure as hell glad that he did. That way, I knew for sure that no harm would come to Kesha behind all this.

Once Bruce finished telling us what we were gonna do with all the devices he had, Ryda and I took Kesha to the mall to do a little shopping. Psycho said he liked a woman that took pride in the way she looked, so after spending a grip in the mall, making sure Kesha was fly as hell, we went to the beauty salon to get our hair, nails, and toes done. Them two lil' hussies hit my pockets hard, but it was well worth it. Besides, I had so much money now that our little outing didn't hurt my pockets at all.

It was just about closing time when we left the mall, and I was tired and hungry as hell. Shopping with them young girls reminded me that I ain't no spring chicken anymore. As we were driving Kesha to my old apartment that she would be staying in while dealing with Cutty, Ryda decided to go over Kesha's back story one more time.

"My name is Holly Graham. I'm twenty-one years old. I was born and raised in Ozark, Alabama but moved to Memphis in my early teens. I attend University of Memphis, and I'm majoring in Health and Sports Science. I want to get into Sports Medicine to be a physical therapist and an athletic trainer," Kesha recited with ease.

Truth be told, her story was almost her actual story, minus her name, age, and where she was born. She was twenty-three, from Grand Junction, Tennessee. She moved to Memphis a few years ago, chasing a nigga that abused her then left her broke and alone. She started stripping to get her started in college. But that was short-lived once she met and started working for Panama. He eventually made her drop out of school and move into the house with the other girls. After his death, I made sure that she enrolled back in school so that she could get her degree and do something better with her life. I wanted the same for Ryda, but with Panama running shit the way he did, I didn't see that as being a possibility for her.

"I think she's ready already, Sunny. What you think?" Ryda inquired.

"Just about. You did great today, Kesha, and with a few more days, you'll be ready," I answered.

"I'll be ready. The money I'm making doing this will pay off my next semester, and I'll be one step closer to getting my degree and getting far away from Tennessee. You picked the right girl for the job."

Ryda and I both looked at Kesha in amazement, and she laughed at the expression on our faces.

"Trust me ladies, Cutty ain't gonna know what hit him," Kesha stated, flashing us a devilish grin, causing Ryda to beam with excitement.

That following weekend, Kesha took a trip to The Arcade Restaurant to get a bite to eat. Psycho told us that Cutty usually went there before heading to the strip club. As she passed by his table, his eyes caught a glimpse of her ass, and he couldn't stop himself from looking. Kesha was walking like Ryda and I had taught her, only she put an extra bounce in the walk to make her ass jiggle a little. As she ordered her food, she leaned over the counter, giving Cutty full view.

"Niggas are nasty as fuck!" Ryda shouted as we watched Cutty eyeing Kesha's ass and licking his lips on the monitor.

"Shit, what's nasty about that? When I saw all that ass you had on yo' back, my ass started drooling too." Psycho chuckled as he leaned his head to the side and took a peek at Ryda's ass.

She playfully slapped him on the forehead. "Freak," she called him as she sat on his lap.

We turned our attention back on the monitor just as Kesha accidently spilled her drink on Cutty.

"What the fuck? Bitch!" Cutty shouted as he jumped up.

"Oh, I'm so sorry! Let me get that for you," she apologized, grabbing a handful of napkins and cleaning his pants as Cutty quickly sat down.

Kesha wiped his pants slowly and upwards towards his manhood. Cutty grabbed her by the wrist.

"You don't have to do that, ma. I'm good," he said.

Without lifting her head, Kesha seductively looked upwards into Cutty's eyes.

"Well, apparently, somebody else think that I do," she spoke in a low, smoky voice as she gave him a smirk.

Psycho burst into laughter. "That weak ass nigga's dick must be getting hard. Who the fuck gets horny form a girl cleaning you off?"

Ryda, turned around and looked at him with raised brows. "Was you watching what she was doing?" she asked.

"Yeah, wiping soda off his pants," he answered.

"Nope." I laughed before continuing. "Yeah, she was wiping him off. At the same time, she was softly rubbing on his dick as she moved her body back and forth, brushing against him lightly."

"And?" he asked with a scrunched face.

"And that means that me and Ryda taught her well. Cutty is not only interested, but he's turned on," I replied, pointing at the monitor.

Psycho moved Ryda to the side a little as he scooted to the edge of his seat then stared at the monitor with narrowed eyes. Suddenly, he let out a slight belly laugh.

"Yeah, nigga, she got you, and so do I," he spoke in a taunting tone as a wicked grin appeared on his face.

CUTTY

"Damn, Holly, you know how to make a nigga feel like a fucking king, don't you?" I questioned in a strangulated voice as I held the smoke from my blunt in my mouth.

Holly was on her knees in front of me, giving me that crucial ass slow head as I sat back on the couch, smoking a blunt.

"Shit!" I hissed as she made my entire dick disappear down her throat. "Baby, I'ma call you the deep throat queen, keep sucking this muthafucka like that."

Holly slowly pulled my rod out of her mouth then licked her lips.

"Daddy, you can call me what you want. You want me to be your deep throat queen, then that's who I'll be," she replied as she stood to her feet.

Holly placed her hands on my knees to support herself as she bent forwards,licking her lips to moisten them.She spat on my dick, then slowly slid my joint deep into her mouth tighting her jaws as she went down. Holly went so far down that part of my balls went into her mouth. I leaned back and thrusted my pelvis forward as I gripped her hair with both hands. I swear, baby girl didn't gag at all. As she continued pulling my rod in and out of her mouth, going deeper while sucking tightly, she started swirling her tongue around my balls.

"Fuck, Holly, you tryna suck the life out of a nigga, damn." I groaned as my toes started tingling.

Holly sped up her pace, taking in every inch of my dick and part of my balls every time she sucked it down her throat.

"I'm about to nut already, baby. Slow that shit down." I grimaced, trying to hold back the explosion that was bound to happen.

Baby girl ignored my ass and kept the pace going as she started humming. The slurping and smacking sounds she made only heightened my arousal. She had my dick so wet that I could feel her spit slowly running down the inside of my thigh. I bit down on my bottom lip and gripped her hair tight as hell as my whole body started trembling.

"Ahhhhh, fuuuuck!" I shouted as I busted down her throat.

Shorty slurped up every drop. And the little bit that escaped, she licked it up.

"Mmm, daddy, you taste so good." She moaned, smacking her lips.

Stretching out as far as I could, trying to recover from that intense nut I just had, I exhaled a deep breath then relit my jay. Holly climbed on top of me, straddling me as she lowered herself down on my Johnson.

"Baby, wait," I commanded, trying to stop her.

My body was still sensitive, and her touch made me quiver. Once again, she ignored my command and continued to slowly grind on my dick in a circular motion. Closing my eyes, I laid my head back against the couch and enjoyed the feeling. I took a pull of the blunt, and she started gently sucking on the middle of my neck, teasing my Adam's apple with her tongue.

"Mmm." I moaned, gripping her fat ass with one hand, bouncing her a little.

Holly grabbed the back of the couch then sped up her pace, making me lose all control. I wasn't used to a bitch handling my long shlong like Holly, and that shit was blowing my fucking mind. I put the blunt in the ashtray, gripped her ass with both hands, and started slamming her down on my rod, hard and fast. Shit, that didn't faze her either. She grabbed my hands, pinning them on the couch and then started grinding back and forth, hard and fast. She had the entire couch rocking, and my ass was trying hard as hell not to scream like a little bitch. I knew I had to do something to take over and show this girl who the fucking man was. Although I loved her aggressiveness, I needed to pound that pussy hard to show her that I wasn't no weak ass nigga. I lifted her off me, pushed her over the arm of the couch, spread her legs, and plowed deep into her from behind.

"Oh, daddy, yes. Fuck me hard!" she yelled as she started throwing her ass back.

I pushed her down more, causing her to plant her hands on the floor for support; then, I lifted her right leg over the back of the couch as I pulled her hair and roughly pounded her box. She was screaming and yelling all types of obscenities, but shit, baby girl was giving back to me as much as I was giving it to her. The sounds of her wetness smacking, our bodies slapping against each other, and our grunts, moans, and shouts filled the air as we continued trying to out fuck each other until we both climaxed and collapsed on the couch. As we laid still on the couch, trying to recover, I couldn't help but to think that I had met my match.

It had only been a little over two weeks since I met her at The Arcade Restaurant. She walked in the door, and all I saw was my dream girl. I'd loved Nia Long ever since I saw her in the movie *Friday*, and Holly was almost her doppelganger. I had to do a double take before I realized that it wasn't her. Then, baby girl walked pass me, and I saw all that ass in those jeans and those sexy ass bowlegs just like Nia Long's; a nigga's dick damn near jumped for joy. Kayo and Cliff noticed the look of awe that was planted on my face and tried to clown me but immediately shut the fuck up when I mugged their asses. Suddenly, I felt a drink fall on my leg, and I was about to spaz on whoever it was, but when I looked up and saw those gorgeous, chestnut eyes and those sexy, plump lips on the face of my dream girl, I quickly calmed the hell down.

"Oh, I'm so sorry. Let me get that for you," she apologized in the most pleasant sounding voice as she started wiping me off.

The way she kept gently brushing my manhood and moving her body in an almost snake-like manner had a nigga wanting to bend her ass over that table and fuck the dog shit out of her. I had to stop her from cleaning me off 'cause I was starting to brick up. Then, I asked her name.

"Holly Graham," she stated, smiling.

"Well, Ms. Holly Graham, it's nice to meet you. My name is Cutty," I introduced.

I offered to buy her a fresh meal if she would join me. She accepted, and I sent Kayo and Cliff away so that Holly and I could get acquainted. Once they left, we started talking, and I found out a lot about Holly. She was twenty-one, born and raised in Ozark, Alabama. She attended the

University of Memphis to get a degree in Health and Sports Science. She wanted to go into Sports Medicine to be a physical therapist and an athletic trainer. I was impressed. Not too many girls that I met and were my age had their shit together like Holly. I saw that she had a good head on her shoulder. I had to have her, and I think that I was already catching feelings for her.

Before I could give her my heart like I wanted to, I had to get my mans, Fred, to run a check on her. I don't trust no fucking body, so I had to make sure baby girl was who she said she was. Just like I'd hoped, Fred said she was legit, but shorty be moving funny. I didn't know if it were her busy schedule with school or what, but I couldn't shake this feeling that Holly wasn't being completely honest with me.

"Baby, move your arm. I got to take a shower so I can go. I got something to do, and I got an early class in the morning," she said, trying to get up.

"So you not gon' stay the night?" I asked.

"Cutty, last time I stayed, I didn't get sleep, and I was late for class. I can't be late again. I'm sorry, but I promise I'll stay the whole weekend with you." She stroked my cheek then kissed me softly.

"Aight, baby, come on. Let's take a shower," I stated as I climbed over her.

After showering, Holly hurried to get dressed and headed out of the door. As soon as she left, I called Kayo and told him to follow her. Holly and I were at my house on Florida Street, and Kayo was two houses down, at the house where I kept my product.

"I'm heading out now. I'll call you and let you know where she goes." We ended the call, and I headed into the living room to finish the blunt that I was smoking.

As I was pouring myself a glass of Cîroc, I noticed that Holly had left her necklace on the table. I picked it up and stated twirling it in my hands.

"Ok, Holly, what the hell did you have to do so important that you had to rush yo' ass out of here so quickly?" I mumbled to myself before gulping down my drink.

I placed the necklace in the glass bowl on the table then poured myself another drink. I picked up my blunt and started smoking it as I sat back and waited for Kayo's call.

About a half an hour and another blunt later, Kayo called. I quickly snatched the phone off the table and answered it.

"Yo, Cutty, I don't know what the fuck going on, but this bitch on some funny shit!" Kayo damn near screamed into the phone. He sounded as if he were a little confused, which made me more anxious to know what the hell he found out.

"Kayo, spit the shit out," I demanded.

"You know that hoe house? The House of Angels?" he asked.

"Yeah, nigga. The little joint Panama use to run," I replied, wondering why the hell he was asking me that question.

"Check this shit out. Yo' girl just went there. She was in there for about fifteen minutes. I followed her to the Marathon Gas Station over there on Elvis Presley Boulevard."

"That joint over there by Yajir's house?"

"Yeah, she got out her car and got into a black truck. I can't see who she's talking to, but the bitch been in there for a few minutes. Oh, wait, she's getting out now. She just pulled off. You want me to keep following her?"

Before I could answer, Kayo started shouting in the phone again.

"Oh, shit! Nigga, guess who the fuck this bitch was talking too in the truck! Nigga, you won't believe this bullshit."

"Who, nigga, who?" I asked as I sat up on the edge of the couch.

"Nigga, muthafuckin' Yajir," he answered.

"What? Nigga, get back to that nigga's house. I'm on my way to snatch that bitch, Holly. If you see that nigga, Yajir, keep eyes on him until I get there. He tried to use a hoe bitch to set me up. If we have to comb the whole damn city, then that's what the fuck we gon' do. I want Yajir's bitch ass dead tonight. If the nigga wake up in the morning, yo' ass is dead."

I hung up the phone, grabbed my piece and some bullets, and headed out the door. Yajir used Holly to try to get at me, now I was gonna use her to put his ass in the ground.

PSYCHO

"Psycho, is everything alright? You know I hate sitting alone, wondering what's going on," Ryda whined, and I shook my head.

"Ryda, chill out. Everything is good. I need you to be calm and wait. I got to pick up Bruce and a stop to make before heading that way. Me and Bruce got some shit to take care of. I need you to be patient. Can you do that for me?" I inquired.

"I'm trying, but—" she began, but I interrupted her.

"But nothing, Ryda. You have to be patient. I'll be there as soon as possible."

Ryda breathed in a deep breath then blew it out before responding.

"Ok, Psycho, I can do that. I just want everything to go as planned. We didn't prepare for the next part of the plan, and I'm praying that it works."

"It will. Trust me. We gon' be good," I assured.

"Alright, baby. I trust you. I know we gonna be good," she said as she let out a sigh of relief.

"Forever my Ryda?" I asked, reminding her of who we were.

"Forever your Ryda. I love you," she replied.

"I love you, too. See you soon." I ended the call then tossed my phone in the passenger seat.

Pulling into Bruce's shop, I noticed Sunny's car parked out front. I eyed it suspiciously, wondering what the hell was she doing there, especially since Bruce and I were about to ride out. I grabbed my phone off the seat and sent him a quick text, telling him that I was outside. I got out of the car then leaned against the hood of the car, waiting for him to open the garage door. When he opened the door, he was standing there with his hand on the small of Sunny's back, leading her out. I looked at the two of them with raised brows, wondering what the hell was going on with the two of them. I'd been noticing them flirting a little here and there, but I didn't think that it would've amounted to anything.

"Go to my house and wait for me to call you. Don't go nowhere else. If you hungry, I got food in the house. You understand?" Bruce quizzed Sunny as he handed her his keys.

"Yes, Bruce, I understand. I'm not a dumbass and I'm no stranger to this shit. I'm leaving here and going straight to your house. I will not pass go, and I will not collect two hundred dollars." Sunny rolled her eyes as she took the keys out of his hand.

"You may not be a dumbass, but you sho' as hell is a smart ass." Bruce chuckled, making Sunny burst into laughter.

Frowning my face, I looked back and forth between the two of them, trying to figure out what the hell was so funny. Apparently, her little reference to the Monopoly game was supposed to be some slick comment, and him calling her a smart ass was funny as hell. I failed to see the humor in either one of their jokes.

"Old people." I snickered, shaking my head.

"Boy, you better watch who you calling old. He may be, but I'm not." Sunny cackled as she got in her car.

She waved to us through the window as we hopped in the truck. Bruce was sitting in the passenger seat with a smirk on his face.

"Everything in place?" Bruce asked, sliding into the passenger's side.

"Yeah, everything is where it's supposed to be," I answered, leaning to the side and looking at him in disbelief.

"What?" he asked, throwing his hands up.

"What? Nigga, what the fucks going on with you and Sunny?" I questioned.

"Grown folks' business; that's what's going on. Now shut up and drive." He chuckled.

I shook my head. "Naw, Bruce, you gon' talk today. I need to know what's up. You know that's breaking the bro code, right?"

"Yeah, but shit, the heart wants what the heart wants, and I been wanting Stephanie long before J.B. even knew she existed. I kept that shit inside all them years, out of love and respect for your father, but seeing her after all these years, looking just as good as she did then, I can't hold that shit in no more."

"Well, Bruce, as much as it kills me to say this, I got to say it. My daddy not here no more and been gone thirteen years. If Sunny feeling you like you feeling her, I say go for it."

Bruce looked me up and down then started laughing.

"Look at you, trying to give me advice." He shook his head. "Trust me, I'm trying to get Stephanie, but she's still stuck on that shit. She still loves your daddy, but I'm not gon' give up. I know she wants me," he continued.

I nodded my head in understanding then gave him dap as we turned onto Elvis Presley Boulevard. Bruce reached under the seat and grabbed his bag.

"Park in that space over there. You go left; I go right," he instructed as I pulled into the parking space and shut the engine off.

We quietly got out of the truck then made our way up to the building. Just as we thought, that nigga Kayo was still camping outside of my crib, keeping eyes on me, or so he thought.

I crouched down and crept up to the driver side of his car.

"You should watch yo' back, muthafucka," I said as I pressed the gun into his head through the rolled down window.

He made a sudden movement to reach for his gun.

"This just ain't yo' day," Bruce taunted, placing his gun through the passenger side window.

"Fuck!" Kayo shouted as he held his head down, shaking it.

"Nigga, get the fuck out the car," I ordered as I yanked open his door then dragged his ass out of the car.   I tossed the nigga on the ground, and stomped him a few times before dragging him to his feet and into the building.

When we got to my apartment, the couple that Bruce had to walk around my apartment, posing as Ryda and I, were already covering my floors and furniture with plastic tarp. Bruce thanked them for their services then paid them the money that he promised him, and they left. I tossed Kayo to the middle of the floor.

"You a dead nigga walking," he taunted, staring at me with a look of disgust.

Whap!

"Shut the fuck up!" I shouted, slapping him with my gun.

Bruce grabbed Kayo up off the floor by his throat.

"Naw, nigga, you gon' take this like a man," he said, making Kayo stand tall.

Looking at that nigga, mugging me and trying to play tough, pissed me off. I punched him in the face, sending him crashing back to the floor.

"Yajir, stop playing with this nigga and get this shit over with. We got shit to handle," Bruce reminded me as he stood Kayo up again.

Kayo's legs were like jelly as he stood there, slowly wobbling back and forth. I put the silencer on my gun, cocked it, and then pressed the barrel right between his eyes. I pulled the trigger. Kayo's body hit the ground like a sack of potatoes. We wrapped him up in the tarp, and then, we took turns in the bathroom, quickly cleaning off the blood and changing clothes. After making sure we'd cleaned everything up and making sure that the coast was clear, we took Kayo's lifeless body and put him in the trunk of his own car. I got in the driver side of Kayo's car, started the engine, and then checked my phone for missed calls or text messages, but there were none.

Good, I thought as Bruce pulled up beside me in the truck then rolled down the window.

"We good?" he asked.

I nodded my head yes, then started the engine in Kayo's car. Bruce pulled off, and I followed closely behind him on our way to our destination.

RYDA

My body couldn't stop shaking as I paced the floor, waiting for the phone to ring. Psycho kept telling me that everything was gonna be alright, but I couldn't help but think that something was going to go wrong. We had everything planned perfectly, then acting on impulse, Psycho changed everything. He wanted to move our plan up and none of us were prepared.

"What the fuck is taking so damn long?" I asked no one in particular as I flopped down on the bed, placing my trembling hands under my legs as I bounced my knees up and down.

I was getting antsy, and sitting on my hands was the only thing I could do to keep myself from picking up the phone and calling Psycho again. He should be on his way, and I really didn't want to keep calling him, worrying him. I stretched across the bed, grabbed my phone, and signed on to the Instagram account that I used to keep eyes on Davion. As soon as I logged on, I saw that I had a message notification. Then name Won_P appeared on the screen along with my brother Anwon's picture.

Nice Pic!!!!!

I bit down on my bottom lip, thinking if I should reply or not. After going back and forth with myself in my head, I decided to reply.

Thanks!!!

You're beautiful. Can we talk?

I exited out of the app then tossed the phone on the bed. Why in the hell would he want to talk to me? The pictures that were posted on my page were some pictures that I took off the internet and photoshopped. Granted, the girl was beautiful, she had to be to get my nasty ass brother to accept my friend request. She was a light-skinned, mixed girl with long, curly hair, green eyes, and a body that was thick in all the right places. I only made the account so that I could keep eyes on Davion. But now, Anwon was on here trying to talk to me. Well, not me, but the girl that he thought I was. I stared at the phone, wondering if I should continue the conversation or not. I hated Anwon and Jalel as much as I hated Raymond, and I wanted nothing to do with either one of them. As far as I was concerned, they could rot in hell with their dead ass daddy.

Suddenly, my phone pinged, alerting me that I received a messaged. I let out a sigh before grabbing it and reading the message.

No response. Is that a no?

I laid my head back against the headboard and closed my eyes.

"Remember your purpose, Ryda?" I coached myself.

I looked down at my phone, and as I was about to respond, my phone vibrated in my hand. Kesha's number was displayed on the screen. I quickly answered it.

"Ryda, I'm in trouble. I need Psycho to come get me." Her voice was tremulous as she spoke in a fearful tone.

"Kesha, what's wrong." I asked as I hopped off the bed.

"It's Cutty. He knows. I need Psycho to come get me—now," she replied.

"He's not here. I'll call him for you. Where are you?" I inquired, but she didn't respond. I called her name several times before she answered.

"I'm here. I'm at my house. But Ryda, I don't have time. I need to leave now!"

I could hear a hint of urgency in her voice as she spoke.

"Ok, Kesha, I'll come get you," I offered.

"Hurry, Ryda, before he gets here. I'm afraid," she sobbed.

I ended the call and immediately called Psycho to let him know what was going on. He didn't answer. My heart started pounding in my chest as I paced back and forth, trying to figure out what to do. I knew that Psycho would be pissed if he knew that I left without telling him. I tried to call him again, but still no answer. I tried to call Sunny to let her know where I was going, but just like Psycho, I got no answer.

"Fuck!" I shouted, thinking that everything we planned has just been fucked up.

"Fuck it," I mumbled to myself as I quickly threw on my shoes,

Ty Leese Javeh

grabbed the keys to the car, and headed out of the door.

As I was pulling out of the driveway, I shot Psycho a text.

Kesha called. I'm heading her way now.

I tossed the phone on the seat as I continued driving down the street.

About ten minutes later, I was pulling into Sunny's old apartment complex. I picked up the phone to see if Psycho had texted me back. I saw that Anwon had sent me several messages on Instagram, but there were no messages from Psycho. As I was putting my phone in my pocket, it pinged, notifying me that I had a message.

"Damn, Anwon, I don't have time for this," I snapped as I opened the messaged to read it.

As a smile appeared on my face, my heart started pounding. The words that I read in that message were the most beautiful words that I ever read. I laid my head back against the seat and took a deep breath. Then, I placed the phone in my pocket and got out of the car. As I was approaching the building, I noticed that all the lights in the apartment were turned off, and it was dark as hell. I wasn't sure if Kesha were still in there, so I decided to give her a call. When she didn't answer, I knew something terrible had happened. I closed my eyes and secretly prayed that I was wrong. I could hear Psycho whispering that everything was going to be fine. I nodded my head as I took a calming breath then headed around the back to see if the sliding door was unlocked.

Sunny's old apartment was on the ground floor, and the sliding door was facing nothing but a bunch of trees. That made it much easier to slip in and slip out without being noticed. I walked up to the door and peeked in to see if I could get a good glimpse of what was going on inside. It was too dark, and the light that was shining on the glass made it more difficult for me to see anything at all. Placing my face between my hands as I held them up to the door to block out the glare from the street lights, I squinted my eyes to see if I could get a better view.

"Kesha," I shouted, noticing her laying still on the couch with her leg and arm hanging off the edge.

I slowly slid the door to the side, and to my surprise, it opened. Looking around and making sure to leave the door open, I quickly made my way over to Kesha.

"Kesha. Kesha!" I called as I shook her.

She didn't move. I checked to see if she was breathing, and she was. I reached up, stroked the side of her cheek, and felt a warm liquid running down her face. I stumbled backwards, almost tripping over the coffee table, realizing that the liquid was blood. My breathing became rapid as tears started to form in my eyes.

"Kesha, I'm sorry," I whispered as I laid my head on her hand.

She placed her other hand on my head. I looked up, and she placed her finger over her mouth.

"Shhhh." She shushed me. "I'm alright. Calm down," she whispered as she started trying to sit up.

I grabbed her around the waist and pulled her into a sitting position.

"You hurt?" I asked as I felt my way in the dark to the lamp beside the couch. I bumped into the table, almost knocking the lamp down.

"I'll be ok," she grunted.

Kesha getting hurt, in any way, wasn't a part of the plan. We all knew it was a risk, but Bruce was supposed to have eyes on her at all times. This was never supposed to happen. Holding the lamp in place, I turned it on.

"Oh, my God, Kesha." I gasped, covering my mouth with my hands as I stared at the sight of a badly beaten Kesha.

She had a small gash on her head and a cut over her already swollen shut eye. Both her nose and her mouth were bloody. I rushed to her side and started examining her bruises.

"This wasn't supposed to happen," I said as my eyes started to well up.

Kesha shook her head. "Don't cry," she whispered.

I nodded my head and quickly wiped the tear that was now falling away.

"Let me get something to clean you up," I said as I started to get up from the couch.

Kesha's eye widened as she grabbed me by the wrist, pulling me back down on the couch as she shook her head no. An eerie feeling crept over me as chills ran down my spine. It was something by the way Kesha kept glancing over my shoulder that alarmed me. Remembering that I'd left the sliding door open, I glanced at it.

"Everything is gonna be ok, Kesha. I promise," I promised.

"You sure about that?" asked a deep voice from behind me.

I closed my eyes, secretly praying that what I was saying was true. I turned around and came face to face with the barrel of a gun.

"Cutty," I said with hatred in my tone.

"You must be Ryda?" he asked, giving me the once over. "Damn, you are a sexy lil' bitch," he added, licking his lips. "Too bad you have to die." He flashed an evil grin as the sound of a gun cocking filled the room.

To be continued...

OTHER WORKS BY THE AUTHOR

Survivor of Love 1 and 2

Adonis and Venus 1,2, and 3

Lovin' You Ain't Good for Me

All I Want Is You

I Need Somebody Down for Me

Committed to Love

CPSIA information can be obtained
at www.ICGtesting.com
Printed in the USA
LVOW13s1222190517
535033LV00027B/875/P